# JACQUES AND HIS MASTER

## Also by Milan Kundera

# MILAN KUNDERA

# JACQUES
# AND HIS MASTER

*An Homage to Diderot
in Three Acts*

*Translated from the French by Michael Henry Heim*

1817

**HARPER & ROW, PUBLISHERS,** New York
*Cambridge, Philadelphia, San Francisco, London
Mexico City, São Paulo, Singapore, Sydney*

English translation copyright © 1985 by Harper & Row, Publishers, Inc. Translated from *Jacques et son maître*, copyright © 1981 by Éditions Gallimard.

*Designer: Sidney Feinberg*

Library of Congress Cataloging in Publication Data

Kundera, Milan.
  Jacques and his master.

  Translation of: Jacques et son maître.
  I. Diderot, Denis, 1713–1784.  II. Heim, Michael Henry.  III. Title.
PG5039.21.U6J313      1985          891.8′625          84–48411
ISBN 0-06-091222-7 (pbk.)

85 86 87 88 89 10 9 8 7 6 5 4 3 2 1

# Contents

# Introduction
# to a Variation

## 1

When in 1968 the Russians occupied my small country, all my books were banned and I suddenly lost all legal means of earning a living. A number of people tried to help me; one day a director came and proposed that I write a stage adaptation, under his name, of Dostoevsky's *The Idiot*.

So I reread *The Idiot* and realized that even if I were starving, I could not do the job. Dostoevsky's universe of overblown gestures, murky depths, and aggressive sentimentality repelled me. All at once I felt an inexplicable pang of nostalgia for *Jacques le Fataliste*.

. "Wouldn't you prefer Diderot to Dostoevsky?"

No, he would not. I, on the other hand, could not shake off my strange desire; to remain in the company of Jacques and his master as long as possible, I began to picture them as characters in a play of my own.

## 2

Why the sudden aversion to Dostoevsky?

Was it the anti-Russian reflex of a Czech traumatized by the occupation of his country? No, because I never stopped loving Chekhov. Was it doubts about the aesthetic value of the work? No, because my aversion had taken me by surprise and made no claims to objectivity.

What irritated me about Dostoevsky was the *climate* of his novels: a universe where everything turns into feeling;

1

in other words, where feelings are promoted to the rank of value and of truth.

On the third day of the occupation, I was driving from Prague to Budejovice (the town where Camus set his play *Le Malentendu*—"The Misunderstanding"). All along the roads, in the fields, in the woods, everywhere, there were encampments of Russian infantrymen. At one point they stopped my car. Three soldiers began searching it. Once the operation was over, the officer who had ordered it asked me in Russian, *"Kak chuvstvuetes?"*—that is, "How do you feel? What are your feelings?" His question was not meant to be malicious or ironic. On the contrary. "It's all a big misunderstanding," he continued, "but it will straighten itself out. You must realize we love the Czechs. We love you!"

The countryside ravaged by thousands of tanks, the future of the country compromised for centuries, Czech government leaders arrested and abducted, and an officer of the occupying army makes you a declaration of love. Please understand me: He had no desire to condemn the invasion, not in the least. They all spoke more or less as he did, their attitude based not on the sadistic pleasure of the ravisher but on quite a different archetype: unrequited love. Why do these Czechs (whom we love so!) refuse to live with us the way we live? What a pity we're forced to use tanks to teach them what it means to love!

### 3

Man cannot do without feelings, but the moment they are considered values in themselves, criteria of truth, justifications for kinds of behavior, they become frightening. The noblest of national sentiments stand ready to justify the greatest of horrors, and man, his breast swelling with lyric fervor, commits atrocities in the sacred name of love.

When feelings supplant rational thought, they become

the basis for an absence of understanding, for intolerance; they become, as Carl Jung has put it, "the superstructure of brutality."

The elevation of sentiment to the rank of a value dates back quite far, perhaps even to the moment when Christianity broke off from Judaism. "Love God and do as you will," said Saint Augustine. The famous saying is revealing: It shifts the criterion for truth from the outside inward, into the arbitrary sphere of the subjective. A vague feeling of love ("Love God!"—the Christian imperative) supplants the clarity of the Law (the imperative of Judaism) to become the rather hazy criterion of morality.

The history of Christian society is an age-old school of feelings: Jesus on the cross taught us to cherish suffering; chivalric verse discovered love; the bourgeois family made us nostalgic for domestic life; political demagoguery has managed to "sentimentalize" the will to power. It is this long history that has fashioned the wealth, strength, and beauty of our feelings.

But from the Renaissance on, this Western sensibility has been balanced by a complementary spirit: that of reason and doubt, of play and the relativity of human affairs. It was then that the West truly came into its own.

In his celebrated Harvard speech, Solzhenitsyn places the starting point of the current crisis of the West squarely in the Renaissance. It is Russia—Russia as a separate civilization—that is explained and revealed by his assessment, for Russia's history differs from the history of the West precisely in its lack of a Renaissance and of the spirit that resulted. That is why the Russian mentality maintains a different balance between rationality and sentiment; in this other balance (or imbalance) we find the famous mystery of the Russian soul (its profundity as well as its brutality).

When this weight of rational irrationality fell on my country, I felt an instinctive need to breathe deeply of the spirit of the post-Renaissance West. And that spirit seemed nowhere more concentrated than in the feast of intelligence, humor, and fantasy that is *Jacques le Fataliste.*

*4*

If I had to define myself, I would say I am a hedonist trapped in a world politicized in the extreme. Such is the situation I depict in *Laughable Loves,* the book of mine I am fondest of because it reflects the happiest period of my life. A strange coincidence: I completed the last of the stories for the book (after working on them all through the sixties) three days before the Russians arrived.

When the French edition appeared in 1970, critics placed it in the tradition of the Enlightenment. Moved by the comparison, I was somewhat childishly eager to confirm that I did in fact love the eighteenth century. To tell the truth, I love not so much the eighteenth century as I do Diderot. And to be more frank, I love his novels. And to be exact, I love *Jacques le Fataliste.*

Such a perception of Diderot's oeuvre may be excessively personal, but it is not, perhaps, unjustified. We can do without Diderot the playwright; we can, if we must, understand the history of philosophy without reading the essays of the great encyclopedist; but—and here I insist— the history of the novel would be incomplete and incomprehensible without *Jacques le Fataliste.* I might go so far as to say that this work suffers from being examined exclusively as part of the Diderot canon rather than in the context of the world novel; its true grandeur becomes apparent only in the company of *Don Quixote* or *Tom Jones,* *Ulysses* or *Ferdydurke.*

But by comparison with Diderot's other activities, wasn't *Jacques le Fataliste* merely an entertainment? And wasn't he strongly influenced by his great model, Laurence Sterne's *Tristram Shandy?*

*5*

I often hear it said that the novel has exhausted all its possibilities. I have the opposite impression: During its four-hundred-year history, the novel has missed many of its possibilities; it has left many great opportunities unexplored, many paths forgotten, calls unheard.

*Tristram Shandy* is one of those great lost opportunities. The novel has made the most of the example of Samuel Richardson, who discovered its psychological possibilities in the epistolary form. It has paid, on the other hand, scant attention to the perspective contained in Sterne's enterprise.

*Tristram Shandy* is a game novel. Sterne dwells at length on the days of his hero's conception and birth only to abandon him shamelessly and all but permanently the moment he comes into the world; he banters with his reader and loses his way in endless digressions; he starts an episode and never finishes it; he inserts the dedication and preface in the middle of the book, and so on and so forth.

In short: Sterne does not construct his story according to the unity of action principle, which has, as a matter of course, been considered intrinsic to the very idea of the novel. For him, the novel, that great game of invented characters, means unlimited liberty of formal invention.

In Sterne's defense an American critic has written: "*Tristram Shandy*, although it is a comedy, is a serious work, and it is serious throughout." What in heaven's name is a serious comedy and what is a comedy that is not? Although the sentence I have quoted is void of sense, it is a perfect example of the panic that grips literary criticism whenever it must face something that does not appear to be serious.

Let me state categorically: No novel worthy of the name takes the world seriously. Moreover, what does it mean "to take the world seriously"? It certainly means this: Believing what the world would have us believe. From *Don Quixote* to *Ulysses*, the novel has challenged what the world would have us believe.

But one might reply: A novel can refuse to believe in what the world would have us believe while keeping faith with its own truth; it need not take the world seriously to be serious itself.

Then I must ask: But what does it mean "to be serious"? A person is serious if he believes in what he would have others believe.

And that is just what *Tristram Shandy* does not do. *Tristram Shandy* is unserious throughout; it does not make us believe in anything: not in the truth of its characters, nor in the truth of its author, nor in the truth of the novel as a literary genre. *Everything* is called into question, *everything* exposed to doubt; *everything* is entertainment (entertainment without shame)—with *everything* which that implies for the form of the novel.

Sterne discovered the immense possibilities for playfulness inherent in the novel, thereby opening a new path for its evolution. But no one heeded his *"invitation au voyage."* No one followed him. No one but Diderot.

He alone was receptive to this call of the new. It would therefore be absurd to discredit his originality. No one contests the originality of a Rousseau, a Laclos, or a Goethe on the grounds that they owe a great deal (they and the evolution of the novel in general) to naive old Richardson. If the similarity between Sterne and Diderot is so striking, it is only because their common enterprise has remained entirely isolated in the history of the novel.

### 6

The differences between *Tristram Shandy* and *Jacques le Fataliste* are no less important than the similarities.

First there is a *difference in temperament:* Ste
his method is one of deceleration; his perspect
of the microscope (he can stop time and isolate
second of life, as Joyce later did).

Diderot is fast; his method is one of acceleratic , nis
perspective is that of the telescope (I know of no opening
of a novel more fascinating than the first pages of *Jacques
le Fataliste:* the virtuoso alternation of registers, the sense
of rhythm, the *prestissimo* of the initial sentences).

Then there is a *difference in structure: Tristram Shandy* is
the monologue of a single narrator, Tristram himself.
Sterne meticulously follows the slightest whim of his bi-
zarre train of thought.

Diderot uses five narrators, who interrupt one another
to tell the novel's stories: the author himself (in dialogue
with his reader), the master (in dialogue with Jacques),
Jacques (in dialogue with his master), the innkeeper (in
dialogue with her guests), and the Marquis des Arcis. The
dominant device of all these individual stories is dialogue
(of unequaled virtuosity). But since the narrators tell their
dialogues in dialogue (dialogues that fit into other dialogues), the novel as a whole is nothing but a big, noisy
conversation.

There is also a *difference in spirit:* Parson Sterne's book
is a compromise between the spirit of freethinking and
the spirit of sentimentality, a nostalgic memory of
Rabelaisian revelry in the antechamber of Victorian mod-
esty.

Diderot's novel is an explosion of impertinent freedom
without self-censorship, of eroticism without sentimental
alibis.

Finally there is a *difference in the degree of realistic illusion:* Sterne disrupts chronology, but anchors events
firmly in time and place. His characters are odd, but fitted
out with everything necessary to make us believe in their
actual existence.

Diderot creates a space never before seen in the history of the novel: a stage without scenery. Where do the characters come from? We do not know. What are their names? That is none of our business. How old are they? No, Diderot does nothing to make us believe that his characters actually exist at a given moment. In all the history of the novel, *Jacques le Fataliste* represents the most radical rejection of realistic illusion and of the aesthetic of the "psychological" novel.

## 7

The digest approach is a faithful reflection of deep-seated tendencies of our time. It makes me think that one day all past culture will be completely rewritten and completely forgotten behind the rewrite. Adaptations of great novels for the screen and stage are nothing more than a kind of *Reader's Digest*.

My point is not to defend the sacrosanct virginity of works of art. Even Shakespeare rewrote works created by others. He did not, however, make adaptations; he used a work as a theme for his own variations, of which he was then sole and sovereign author. Diderot borrowed from Sterne the entire story of Jacques's being wounded in the knee, taken away in a cart, and cared for by a beautiful woman. But in so doing he neither imitated nor adapted him. He wrote a variation on a theme by Sterne.

On the other hand, the reworkings of *Anna Karenina* one sees on the stage or screen are adaptations, that is, reductions. The more the adapter tries to remain discreetly hidden behind the novel, the more he betrays it. By reducing it, he deprives it not only of its charm but also of its meaning.

Tolstoy, to go no further, posed the issue of human action in a manner radically new in the history of the novel; he discovered the fatal importance of rationally elusive causes in decision-making. Why does Anna commit suicide? Tolstoy goes so far as to use an almost Joycean interior monologue to delineate the network of irrational motivations which drives his heroine to it. Every adaptation of this novel must, by the very nature of the digest approach, attempt to make the causes of Anna's behavior clear and logical, to rationalize them; the adaptation thus becomes the negation, pure and simple, of the novel's originality.

And conversely: If the meaning of a novel survives the rewriting process, it is indirect proof of the novel's mediocrity. In all literature there are two novels that are absolutely irreducible, totally unrewritable: *Tristram Shandy* and *Jacques le Fataliste*. How can one simplify such brilliant disorder and be left with anything? What would be left?

True, one might remove the story of Madame de La Pommeraye and turn it into a play or film; indeed, it has been done. But all that comes of it is a banal anecdote completely lacking in charm. For the beauty of the tale is inseparable from the manner in which Diderot tells it: (1) a woman of the people relates a series of events that take place in a social setting beyond her ken; (2) all possibility of melodramatic identification with the characters is thwarted by the fact that the tale is repeatedly and incongruously interrupted by other anecdotes and remarks and (3) constantly reviewed, analyzed, discussed; but (4) each of the commentators draws a different conclusion from it, since Madame de La Pommeraye's tale is an antimorality.

Why go into all this? Because I wish to cry out with Jacques's master, "Death to all who dare rewrite what has been written! ... Castrate them and cut off their ears!"

*8*

And, of course, to state that *Jacques and His Master* is not an adaptation; it is my own play, my own "variation on Diderot," or, since it was conceived in admiration, my "homage to Diderot."

This "variation-homage" represents a multiple encounter: an encounter of two writers but also of two centuries. And of the novel and the theater. The form of a dramatic work has always been a good deal more rigid and normative than that of the novel. The theater has never had its Laurence Sterne. By trying to endow my comedy with the formal freedom that Diderot the novelist discovered and Diderot the playwright never knew, I have written not only an "homage to Diderot" but also an "homage to the novel."

This is its architecture: On the fragile base of the journey of Jacques and his master rest three love stories: of the master, of Jacques, and of Madame de La Pommeraye. While the first two are loosely (the second only very loosely) connected with the outcome of the journey, the third, which takes up the entire second act, is from the technical standpoint purely and simply an episode (unintegrated as it is into the main action); it is an obvious infringement on the "laws" of dramatic structure. But that was where I made my wager:

Renouncing strict unity of action, I sought to create a coherent whole by more subtle means: by the technique of polyphony (the three stories are intermingled rather than told consecutively) and the technique of variation (each of the three stories is in fact a variation on the others). (And so this play, which is a "variation on Diderot," is simultaneously an "homage to the technique of variation," as was, seven years later, my novel *The Book of Laughter and Forgetting.)*

9

For a Czech writer in the nineteen seventies, it was odd to think that *Jacques le Fataliste* (also written in the seventies) was never published during its author's lifetime and that it circulated among a private and restricted audience in manuscript only. What in Diderot's day was an exception has, in Prague two hundred years later, become the lot of all important Czech writers, who, banned from the presses, can see their works only in typescript. It began with the Russian invasion, it has continued to the present and, by the look of things, is here to stay.

I wrote *Jacques and His Master* for my private pleasure and perhaps with the vague idea that it could one day be put on in a Czech theater under an assumed name. By way of a signature I dotted the text (another game, another variation!) with several mementos of my previous works: Jacques and his master are reminiscent of the two friends in "The Golden Apple of Eternal Desire" *(Laughable Loves);* there is an allusion to *Life Is Elsewhere* and another to *The Farewell Party.* Yes, they were mementos; the entire play was a farewell to my life as a writer, a "farewell in the form of an entertainment." *The Farewell Party,* the novel I completed at approximately the same time, was to have been my last novel. Yet I lived out that period without the bitter taste of personal defeat, my private farewell merging completely with another, immensely greater one, one that went far beyond me:

Faced with the eternity of the Russian night, I had experienced in Prague the violent end of Western culture such as it was conceived at the dawn of the modern age, based on the individual and his reason, on pluralism of thought, and on tolerance. In a small Western country I experienced the end of the West. That was the grand farewell.

*10*

With an illiterate peasant for a servant, Don Quixote set off one day to do battle with his enemies. One hundred and fifty years later, Toby Shandy turned his garden into a great mock-up of a battlefield; there he devoted his time to reminiscing about his youth in the military, faithfully attended by his man, Corporal Trim. Trim walked with a limp, much like Jacques, who ten years later entertained his master on their journey. He was as garrulous and obstinate as the soldier Svejk, who, one hundred and fifty years later, in the Austro-Hungarian army, so amused and horrified his master, Lieutenant Lukac. Thirty years after that, waiting for Godot, Vladimir and his servant are alone on the empty stage of the world. The journey is over.

Servant and master have made their way across all the modern history of the West. In Prague, city of the grand farewell, I heard their fading laughter. With love and anguish, I clung to that laughter as one clings to fragile, perishable things, things that have been condemned.

*Paris, July 1981*

JACQUES AND HIS MASTER

# CHARACTERS

JACQUES
JACQUES'S MASTER
INNKEEPER
CHEVALIER DE SAINT-OUEN
YOUNG BIGRE
OLD BIGRE
JUSTINE
MARQUIS
MOTHER
DAUGHTER
AGATHE
AGATHE'S MOTHER
AGATHE'S FATHER
POLICE OFFICER
BAILIFF

The play should be performed without intermission.

I imagine JACQUES as a man of at least forty. His MASTER is the same age or somewhat younger.

François Germond, who directed the excellent production in Geneva, had an interesting idea: When JACQUES and his MASTER meet again at the beginning of Act Three, Scene 6, they are already old; years have passed since the preceding scene.

The stage remains the same throughout the play. It is divided in two: a downstage area, below, and a raised upstage area, in the form of a large platform. All action taking place in the present is performed downstage; episodes from the past are performed on the upstage platform.

As far upstage as possible (and therefore on the platform) is a staircase (or ladder) leading to an attic.

Most of the time, the set (which should be utterly plain and abstract) is completely bare. For certain episodes, however, actors bring on chairs, a table, etc.

The set must avoid all ornamental, illustrative, and symbolic elements. These are contrary to the spirit of the play, as is any exaggeration in the acting.

The action takes place in the eighteenth century, but in the eighteenth century as we dream of it today. Just as the language of the play does not aim to reproduce the language of the time, so the setting and costumes must not stress the period. The historicity of the characters (especially the two protagonists), though never in question, should be slightly muted.

# ACT ONE

## *Scene 1*

*Enter* JACQUES *and his* MASTER. *After they have taken a few steps,* JACQUES *gazes at the audience. He stops short.*

JACQUES *(discreetly)*: Sir . . . *(pointing out the audience to him)* why are they staring at us?

MASTER *(a bit taken aback and adjusting his clothes as if afraid of calling attention to himself by a sartorial oversight)*: Pretend there's no one there.

JACQUES *(to the audience)*: Wouldn't you rather look somewhere else? All right then, what do you want to know? Where we've come from? *(He stretches his right arm out behind him.)* Back there. Where we're going? *(Philosophically.)* Which of us knows where we're going? *(To the audience.)* Do you know where you're going?

MASTER: I'm afraid, Jacques, that *I* know where we're going.

JACQUES: Afraid?

MASTER *(sadly)*: Yes. But I have no intention of acquainting you with my painful obligations. . . .

JACQUES: None of us knows where we're going, sir, believe me. But as my captain used to say, "It's all written on high. . . ."

MASTER: And right he was. . . .

JACQUES: Damn Justine and that vile attic where I lost my virginity!

MASTER: Why curse the woman, Jacques?

JACQUES: Because the day I lost my virginity, I went out

17

and got drunk. My father, mad with rage, gave me a beating. A regiment was passing through, I signed up, a battle broke out, a bullet hit me in the knee. And that was the start of a long string of adventures. Without that bullet, I don't think I'd ever have fallen in love.

MASTER: You mean you've been in love? You've never told me that before.

JACQUES: There are many things I haven't told you.

MASTER: But how did you fall in love? Tell me that!

JACQUES: Where was I? Oh, yes, the bullet in my knee. I was buried under a pile of dead and wounded bodies. Next day they found me and tossed me in a cart. The road to the hospital was bad, and I howled in pain at the slightest bump. Suddenly we stopped. I asked to be let down. We were at the edge of a village, and I'd noticed a young woman standing in the doorway of a hut. . . .

MASTER: Aha! Now I see. . . .

JACQUES: She went inside, came out with a bottle of wine, and held it to my lips. They tried to load me back in the cart, but I grabbed the woman's skirt. Then I passed out, and when I came to I was inside the hut, her husband and children crowding around me while she applied compresses.

MASTER: You scoundrel, you! I see how it ended!

JACQUES: You don't see a thing, sir.

MASTER: A man welcomes you into his house, and look how you repay him!

JACQUES: But are we the masters of our actions? As my captain used to say, "The good and evil we encounter here below are written first on high." Dear Master, do you know any way of erasing what has been written? Can I cease to be? Can I be someone else? And if I am myself, can I do anything other than what I do?

MASTER: There's something that's been bothering me: Are you a scoundrel because it's written on high? Or was it written on high because they knew you were a scoundrel? Which is the cause, which the effect?

JACQUES: I don't know, sir, but you mustn't call me a scoundrel . . .

MASTER: A man who cuckolds his benefactor . . .

JACQUES: . . . or that man my benefactor. You should have heard the names he called his wife for taking pity on me.

MASTER: And right he was . . . Tell me, Jacques, what was she like? Describe her to me.

JACQUES: The young woman?

MASTER: Yes.

JACQUES *(after a moment of hesitation)*: Average height . . .

MASTER *(not too pleased)*: Hm . . .

JACQUES: Though actually on the tall side . . .

MASTER *(nodding his approval)*: On the tall side . . .

JACQUES: Yes.

MASTER: Just the way I like them.

JACQUES *(making graphic use of his hands)*: Beautiful breasts.

MASTER: Bigger in front or behind?

JACQUES *(hesitating)*: In front.

MASTER *(sadly)*: What a shame.

JACQUES: So you love big bottoms?

MASTER: Yes . . . Big ones like Agathe's . . . And her eyes? What were they like?

JACQUES: Her eyes? I don't remember. But she had black hair.

MASTER: Agathe was blond.

JACQUES: Is it my fault she didn't look like your Agathe? You'll have to take her as she is. But she did have beautiful long legs.

MASTER *(dreamily)*: Long legs. That makes me so happy!

JACQUES: And a majestic bottom.

MASTER: Majestic? Really?

JACQUES *(showing him)*: Like this . . .

MASTER: You scoundrel, you! The more you tell me about her, the wilder I get. . . . The wife of your benefactor, and you went and . . .

JACQUES: No, sir. Nothing ever happened between us.

MASTER: Then why bring her up? Why waste our time with her?

JACQUES: You keep interrupting me, sir. It's a very bad habit.

MASTER: And I already wanted her. . . .

JACQUES: I tell you I'm in bed with a bullet in my knee, suffering agonies, and all you can think about is your lusts. And Agathe, whoever she is.

MASTER: Don't mention that name.

JACQUES: You mentioned it first.

MASTER: Have you ever wanted a woman desperately, only to be rejected by her? Again and again?

JACQUES: Yes. Justine.

MASTER: Justine? The girl you lost your virginity with?

JACQUES: The same.

MASTER: Tell me about her. . . .

JACQUES: After you, sir.

# *Scene 2*

*Several characters have taken their places on the upstage platform.* YOUNG BIGRE *is sitting on the steps;* JUSTINE *is standing next to him. On the opposite side of the stage,* AGATHE *is sitting on a chair that the* CHEVALIER DE SAINT-OUEN *has brought out for her; the* CHEVALIER *is standing at her side.*

SAINT-OUEN *(calling to the* MASTER*)*: Greetings, my friend!

JACQUES *(turning, together with the* MASTER, *and indicating* AGATHE *with his head)*: Is she the one? *(The* MASTER *nods.)* And the man next to her? Who is he?

MASTER: A friend, the Chevalier de Saint-Ouen. He's the one who introduced me to her. *(He looks up at* JUSTINE.*)* And the other one, is she yours?

JACQUES: Yes, but I like yours better.

MASTER: And I prefer yours. More flesh. How about swapping?

JACQUES: You should have thought of that earlier. It's too late now.

MASTER *(with a sigh)*: Yes, too late. And who's the brawny fellow?

JACQUES: Bigre, an old pal. We both wanted her, that girl. But for some mysterious reason, he's the one who got her.

MASTER: My problem exactly.

SAINT-OUEN (*moving toward the* MASTER, *to the edge of the platform*): You might be a bit more discreet, old boy. The parents are fearful of their daughter's reputation. . . .

MASTER (*to* JACQUES, *with indignation*): The filthy shop-keepers! They were perfectly happy to let me shower her with gifts!

SAINT-OUEN: No, no, you don't understand! They have great respect for you. They simply want you to state your intentions. Otherwise you'll have to stop going there.

MASTER (*to* JACQUES, *with indignation*): When I think that he's the one who introduced me to her! Who egged me on! Who promised me she'd be easy!

SAINT-OUEN: I'm merely passing on their message, my friend.

MASTER (*to* SAINT-OUEN): Very well. (*He mounts the platform.*) Then please pass on my message to them: Don't count on dragging me to the altar just yet. As for Agathe, tell her she had best be more tender with me in the future if she doesn't wish to lose me. I have no intention of wasting my time and money on her when I can put them to better use elsewhere.

(SAINT-OUEN *hears him out, bows, and returns to his place beside* AGATHE.)

JACQUES: Bravo, sir! That's how I like you! Brave for a change.

MASTER (*to* JACQUES, *from the platform*): I have my moments. I stopped seeing her.

SAINT-OUEN (*moving back to the* MASTER *along a semicir-*

*cle):* I've passed on your message word for word, but I can't help thinking you were a bit cruel.

JACQUES: My master? Cruel?

SAINT-OUEN: Hold your tongue, boy! *(To the* MASTER.*)* The whole family is horrified by your silence. And Agathe . . .

MASTER: Agathe?

SAINT-OUEN: Agathe weeps.

MASTER: She weeps.

SAINT-OUEN: She spends her days weeping.

MASTER: And so you feel that if I resumed my visits . . .

SAINT-OUEN: It would be a mistake! You can't retreat. You'd lose everything by going back to them now. You must teach those merchants some manners.

MASTER: But what if they never ask me back?

SAINT-OUEN: They will.

MASTER: And if it takes a long time?

SAINT-OUEN: Do you wish to be master or slave?

MASTER: So she's weeping . . .

SAINT-OUEN: Better she than you.

MASTER: And if they never ask me back?

SAINT-OUEN: They will, I tell you. Now make the most of the situation. Agathe must be made to see that you're not ready to eat out of her hand and that she must make an effort. . . . But tell me . . . We're friends, aren't we? Give me your word of honor. Have you and she . . .

MASTER: No.

SAINT-OUEN: Your discretion does you credit.

MASTER: Not in the least. It's the plain truth.

SAINT-OUEN: What? Not one small moment of weakness?

MASTER: Not one.

SAINT-OUEN: I wonder if you haven't behaved too much like a virgin with her.

MASTER: And you, Chevalier? Have you never desired her?

SAINT-OUEN: Of course I have. But the moment you came along, I became invisible to Agathe. Oh, we're still good friends, but nothing more. My only consolation is that if my best friend sleeps with her, I'll feel just as if I myself were doing it. Take my word for it. I'll do my utmost to put you in her bed.

*(At the end of the speech, he moves slowly back to the chair that* AGATHE *is still sitting on.)*

JACQUES: Have you noticed what a good listener I am, sir? I haven't interrupted you once. If only you'd follow my example.

MASTER: You boast about not interrupting me only to interrupt me.

JACQUES: I butt in because you've set a bad example.

MASTER: As master I have the right to interrupt my servant as often as I please. My servant has no right to interrupt his master.

JACQUES: I don't interrupt you, sir; I talk to you, the way you've always asked me to. And let me tell you: I don't like that friend of yours, and I'll bet it's his mistress he wants you to marry.

MASTER: Enough! I have no more to say! *(He steps down from the platform in a huff.)*

JACQUES: No, sir! Please! Go on!

MASTER: What's the use? Your insights are conceited and tasteless; you know everything in advance.

JACQUES: You're right, sir, but do go on. All I've guessed is the barest outline of the story. I can't begin to imagine the charming details of your talks with Saint-Ouen and all the twists and turns of the plot.

MASTER: You've upset me. I refuse to say another word.

JACQUES: Please!

MASTER: If you wish to make peace, you must tell me *your* story. Then I can interrupt as often as I please. What I want to hear is how you lost your virginity, and you can be certain I'll interrupt you a few times during your first act of love.

# *Scene 3*

JACQUES: As you wish, sir; as is your privilege. Look. *(He turns and points to the staircase that* JUSTINE *and* YOUNG BIGRE *are climbing;* OLD BIGRE *is standing at its foot.)* This is the shop where my godfather, Old Bigre, sells the wheels he makes. The ladder goes to the attic, and my friend, Young Bigre, has his bed up there.

OLD BIGRE *(calling up to the attic)*: Bigre! Bigre, you damned do-nothing!

JACQUES: Old Bigre had his bed downstairs, in the shop. Every night after he was sound asleep, Young Bigre would softly open the door and sneak Justine up the ladder with him.

OLD BIGRE: The morning bells have rung, and you're still

snoring away. Do you want me to go up there with a broom and sweep you out?

JACQUES: They'd had such a good time that night they overslept.

YOUNG BIGRE *(from the attic)*: Calm down, Father!

OLD BIGRE: The farmer will be here soon for the axle. Get a move on!

YOUNG BIGRE: Coming! *(He runs down the stairs, buttoning his trousers.)*

MASTER: So she had no way out?

JACQUES: None. She was trapped.

MASTER *(laughing)*: And shaking in her shoes, I imagine.

OLD BIGRE: Ever since he fell for that little slut, he's been snoring half the day away. I wouldn't mind so much if she were worth the trouble. But *that* wench! If his poor mother could have seen them, she'd have long since given him a trouncing and scratched the slut's eyes out in front of the church after mass! But I put up with it, like an idiot. Well, it's time things changed around here! *(To* YOUNG BIGRE.*)* Take this axle, and go and deliver it to the farmer! *(Exit* YOUNG BIGRE *with the axle on his shoulder.)*

MASTER: And Justine heard every word up there?

JACQUES: Naturally!

OLD BIGRE: Damn it to hell, where's my pipe? I bet that good for nothing of mine took it! Let's see if it isn't up in the attic. *(He climbs the stairs.)*

MASTER: And Justine? Justine?

JACQUES: She slipped under the bed.

MASTER: And Young Bigre?

JACQUES: As soon as he'd delivered the axle, he ran over to my house. "Listen," I told him, "go and take a walk around the village. In the meantime, I'll find a way to keep your father busy so Justine can escape. Just be sure to give me enough time." *(He mounts the platform. The* MASTER *smiles.)* What are you smiling about?

MASTER: Oh, nothing.

OLD BIGRE *(who has come down from the loft)*: Godson Jacques! Good to see you! What brings you here so bright and early?

JACQUES: I'm on my way home.

OLD BIGRE: Well, well, Jacques, my boy. Getting to be quite the rake!

JACQUES: What can I say?

OLD BIGRE: You and my son both, I'm afraid. Out all night, eh?

JACQUES: What can I say?

OLD BIGRE: With a whore?

JACQUES: Yes. But with my father I can't even mention the subject!

OLD BIGRE: Which is perfectly understandable. He owes you the same sound beating I owe my son. But how about some breakfast? Wine gives good counsel.

JACQUES: Sorry, Godfather, I can't. I'm dead tired.

OLD BIGRE: Gave it your all, eh? I hope it was worth it. Look, I have an idea. My son is out. Why don't you go up to the attic and stretch out on his bed? *(*JACQUES *climbs the stairs.)*

MASTER *(calling up to* JACQUES*)*: Traitor! Scoundrel! I should have guessed!

OLD BIGRE: Oh, children! . . . Damned children! . . . *(Noises and muffled cries come from the attic.)* Poor boy, some dream he's having. . . . He must have had a rough night.

MASTER: Dream! Ha! He's not dreaming! He's terrorizing her! She tries hard to fight him off, but since she's afraid of being caught, she keeps her mouth shut. You scoundrel, you! You should be tried for rape!

JACQUES *(looking down from the attic)*: I don't know, sir, if I raped her or not. What I do know is that we had rather a good time, the two of us. All she asked me was to promise . . .

MASTER: What did you promise, you villain?

JACQUES: Never to breathe a word of it to Young Bigre.

MASTER: Which gave you the right to go at it again.

JACQUES: And again!

MASTER: How many times?

JACQUES: Many times, and each better than the last.

*(Enter YOUNG BIGRE.)*

OLD BIGRE: What took you so long? Here, take this rim and finish it outside.

YOUNG BIGRE: Outside? Why?

OLD BIGRE: So as not to wake up Jacques.

YOUNG BIGRE: Jacques?

OLD BIGRE: Yes, Jacques. He's up in the attic, taking a nap. Oh, a father's lot! You're all scoundrels, every last one of you. Well, what are you waiting for? Get a move on! *(*YOUNG BIGRE *tears over to the stairs and is about to start climbing.)* Where are you going? Let the poor fellow sleep!

YOUNG BIGRE *(loudly)*: Father! Father!

OLD BIGRE: He was dead tired!

YOUNG BIGRE: I'm going up there!

OLD BIGRE: No, you're not! Do you like it when someone wakes you?

MASTER: And Justine heard all that?

JACQUES *(sitting at the head of the stairs)*: As clearly as you hear me now.

MASTER: Oh, that's wonderful! The perfect scoundrel! And what did you do?

JACQUES: I laughed.

MASTER: You gallows bird! And Justine?

JACQUES: Tore her hair, raised her eyes to heaven, wrung her hands.

MASTER: You're a brute, Jacques. A brute with a heart of stone.

JACQUES *(coming down the stairs, highly serious)*: No, sir, no. I am a man of great sensitivity. But I reserve it for the proper occasions. Those who squander their sensitivity have none left when there's a need for it.

OLD BIGRE *(to JACQUES)*: Ah, there you are! Had a good nap? You really needed one. *(To YOUNG BIGRE.)* He looks as fresh as a daisy now. Go get a bottle from the cellar. *(To JACQUES.)* Now you feel like having some breakfast, don't you?

JACQUES: Do I!

*(YOUNG BIGRE comes back with a bottle, and OLD BIGRE fills three glasses.)*

YOUNG BIGRE *(pushing away his glass)*: I'm not thirsty this early in the morning.

OLD BIGRE: You don't want anything to drink?

YOUNG BIGRE: No.

OLD BIGRE: Ah! I know what it is. *(To* JACQUES.*)* Justine's at the bottom of this. He was out a long time just now. He must have stopped off at her place and caught her with somebody else. *(To* YOUNG BIGRE.*)* Serves you right! I told you she was nothing but a whore! *(To* JACQUES.*)* And now he wants to take it out on an innocent bottle!

JACQUES: You may just be right.

YOUNG BIGRE: This is no laughing matter, Jacques.

OLD BIGRE: Well, we can drink even if he won't. *(Raising his glass.)* Your health, Godson Jacques!

JACQUES *(raising his glass)*: Your health! *(To* YOUNG BIGRE.*)* And you, my friend, have a drink with us. Whatever it is that's bothering you can't be all that bad.

YOUNG BIGRE: I told you, I'm not drinking.

JACQUES: By the next time you see her, the whole thing will have blown over. You have nothing to fear.

OLD BIGRE: Well, I hope she makes him suffer. . . . And now let me take you back to your father and ask him to forgive you your escapades. Damned children! You're all the same! You filthy beasts . . . Let's go. *(He takes* JACQUES *by the arm and starts off with him.* YOUNG BIGRE *runs up the stairs to the attic.* JACQUES *disengages himself after several steps and turns toward his* MASTER. *Exit* OLD BIGRE, *alone.)*

MASTER: An admirable story, Jacques! It teaches us to know our women better—and our friends.

*(*SAINT-OUEN *appears on the platform, which he crosses slowly in the direction of the* MASTER.*)*

JACQUES: Did you really think a friend of yours would give up a chance at your mistress?

# Scene 4

SAINT-OUEN: Friend! Dear friend! Come . . . *(He is at the edge of the platform, holding out his arms to the* MASTER, *who is at its foot. The* MASTER *mounts the platform, and there he joins* SAINT-OUEN, *who takes him by the arm and promenades back and forth with him.)* Ah, how wonderful, dear friend, to have a friend for whom one feels true friendship. . . .

MASTER: I'm touched, Saint-Ouen.

SAINT-OUEN: Indeed, I have no friend who is a better friend than you, dear friend, while I . . .

MASTER: You? You, kind friend, are likewise the best of friends.

SAINT-OUEN *(shaking his head)*: I'm afraid you don't know me at all, my friend.

MASTER: I know you as I know myself.

SAINT-OUEN: If you knew me, you wouldn't want to know me.

MASTER: How can you say such a thing!

SAINT-OUEN: I'm despicable. Yes, that's the word, and I have no choice but to apply it to myself: I am a despicable man.

MASTER: I refuse to let you slander yourself in my presence!

SAINT-OUEN: Despicable!

MASTER: No!

SAINT-OUEN: Despicable!

MASTER *(kneeling before him)*: Hold your tongue, my friend. Your words are breaking my heart. Why torture yourself so? Why reproach yourself?

SAINT-OUEN: My past is tarnished. Merely a single stain, yes, but. . . .

MASTER: You see? What harm can there be in a single stain?

SAINT-OUEN: A single stain can sully an entire life.

MASTER: One swallow does not make a summer. A single stain is no stain at all.

SAINT-OUEN: Oh, no. Single, solitary stain though it be, it's odious. I—I, Saint-Ouen—have betrayed, yes, betrayed a friend!

MASTER: Come now! How did it happen?

SAINT-OUEN: The two of us were pursuing the same young woman. He was in love with her and she was in love with me. While he kept her, I took my pleasure. I never had the courage to admit it to him. But now I must. The next time I see him, I must tell him all, confess to him, unburden myself of the frightful secret. . . .

MASTER: Yes, you must, Saint-Ouen.

SAINT-OUEN: Is that what you advise?

MASTER: I do.

SAINT-OUEN: And how do you think my friend will respond?

MASTER: He'll be touched by your sincerity and remorse. He'll embrace you.

SAINT-OUEN: Do you think so?

MASTER: I do.

SAINT-OUEN: And that is how you yourself would respond?

MASTER: I? Certainly.

SAINT-OUEN *(opening his arms)*: Then embrace me, my friend!

MASTER: What do you mean?

SAINT-OUEN: Embrace me! The friend I've deceived is you!

MASTER *(devastated)*: Agathe?

SAINT-OUEN: Yes . . . Ah, your face has fallen! I give you back your word! Yes, yes! You may do with me as you see fit. You're right. What I did is unforgivable. Leave me! Abandon me! Despise me! Ah, if only you knew what that bitch has done to me, how I've suffered from the treacherous role she forced me into.

# Scene 5

*The two dialogues proceed simultaneously.*

YOUNG BIGRE *and* JUSTINE *come down the stairs and sit side by side on the lowest step. They both seem devastated.*

JUSTINE: But I swear to you! I swear by my father and mother both!

YOUNG BIGRE: I'll never believe you!

*(*JUSTINE *bursts into tears.)*

MASTER *(to* SAINT-OUEN*)*: The bitch! And you, Saint-Ouen, how could you. . . .

SAINT-OUEN: Don't torture me, my friend!

JUSTINE: I swear he never touched me!

YOUNG BIGRE: Liar!

MASTER: How could you?

YOUNG BIGRE: With that swine!

*(*JUSTINE *bursts into tears.)*

SAINT-OUEN: How could I? I'm the most despicable man under the sun! Here I have the best of men for a friend, and I betray him shamefully. And you ask me why? Because I'm a swine! Nothing but a swine!

JUSTINE: He's no swine! He's your friend!

YOUNG BIGRE *(angrily)*: My friend?

JUSTINE: Yes, friend! He never touched me!

YOUNG BIGRE: Shut up!

SAINT-OUEN: Yes, nothing but a swine!

MASTER: No. Stop spitting on yourself!

SAINT-OUEN: But I must spit on myself!

MASTER: No matter what's happened, you must not spit on yourself.

JUSTINE: He told me he was your friend and there could never be anything between us, even if we were alone on a desert island.

MASTER: Stop torturing yourself.

YOUNG BIGRE: He really said that?

JUSTINE: Yes!

SAINT-OUEN: I want to feel pain.

MASTER: We are both victims of the same beast, you and I! She seduced you! You've been so sincere, you've kept nothing from me. You're still my friend!

YOUNG BIGRE: Did he say: "Even on a desert island"?

JUSTINE: Yes!

SAINT-OUEN: I'm unworthy of your friendship.

MASTER: On the contrary. Your pain makes you worthy. You've earned it with the torture of your remorse!

YOUNG BIGRE: Did he really say he was my friend and wouldn't touch you even if you were alone on a desert island?

JUSTINE: Yes!

SAINT-OUEN: Ah, how generous you are!

MASTER: Embrace me! *(They embrace.)*

YOUNG BIGRE: Did he really say he wouldn't touch you even if you were alone on a desert island?

JUSTINE: Yes!

YOUNG BIGRE: On a desert island? Swear to it!

JUSTINE: I swear!

MASTER: Come, let's have a drink!

JACQUES: Oh, sir, I feel sorry for you!

MASTER: To our friendship, which no tart can destroy!

YOUNG BIGRE: On a desert island. I've been very unfair to him. He's a true friend!

JACQUES: Our adventures, Master, seem strangely similar.

MASTER *(leaving his role)*: What was that?

JACQUES: I said that our adventures were strangely similar.

YOUNG BIGRE: Jacques is a true friend.

JUSTINE: Your best friend.

SAINT-OUEN: All I can think of now is revenge! And since the bitch has abused the two of us, we must avenge ourselves together! You have only to give the command— tell me what I must do!

MASTER *(more interested in* JACQUES *and his story, to* SAINT-OUEN*):* Later. We'll finish this story later. . . .

SAINT-OUEN: No, no! Immediately! I'll do anything you ask! Tell me what you have in mind.

MASTER: Yes, yes, but later. Now I want to see how things turn out for Jacques. *(He steps down from the platform.)*

YOUNG BIGRE: Jacques! *(*JACQUES *jumps up on the platform and goes over to* YOUNG BIGRE.*)* Thank you. You're my best friend. *(He embraces him.)* And now embrace Justine. *(*JACQUES *holds back.)* Don't be shy. When I'm around, you have the right to embrace her! I order you to! *(*JACQUES *embraces* JUSTINE.*)* We'll be the best of friends, the three of us, friends for life. . . . On a desert island . . . You mean you really wouldn't touch her? Not even on a desert island?

JACQUES: If she belonged to a friend? Are you out of your mind?

YOUNG BIGRE: You're a true friend!

MASTER: The scoundrel! *(*JACQUES *turns toward his* MASTER.*)* But *my* story is still far from over. . . .

JACQUES: So being cuckolded wasn't enough for you?

YOUNG BIGRE *(overjoyed)*: The truest of women! The truest

of friends! I'm as happy as a king! *(During these lines,* YOUNG BIGRE *exits with* JUSTINE. SAINT-OUEN *remains for the first few lines of the following scene, then exits as well.)*

# Scene 6

MASTER: My story ended badly. With the worst of endings a human story can have . . .

JACQUES: And what is the worst of endings of a human story?

MASTER: Think it over.

JACQUES: Let me think . . . What is the worst of endings of a human story . . . But my story isn't over yet either, sir. I lost my virginity, I found my best friend. I was so happy I went out and got drunk. My father gave me a beating. A regiment was passing through, I signed up, a battle broke out, a bullet hit me in the knee, I was loaded into a cart, the cart stopped in front of a hut, and a woman appeared on the threshold. . . .

MASTER: You've been through that before.

JACQUES: Butting in again, are you?

MASTER: Go on, go on!

JACQUES: I will not! I refuse to be constantly interrupted.

MASTER *(testily)*: All right, but let's keep going. We've still got a long way to go. . . . Wait a minute, damn it! Why is it we have no horses?

JACQUES: You forget that we're on stage. You can't have horses on stage!

MASTER: You mean I have to walk because of a ridiculous play? The master who invented us meant us to have horses!

JACQUES: That's a risk you take when you're invented by too many masters.

MASTER: You know, I've often wondered whether or not we're good inventions. What do you think, Jacques? Are we well invented?

JACQUES: By whom, sir? The one on high?

MASTER: It was written on high that someone here below would write our story, and I can't help wondering whether he did a good job. Was he at least talented?

JACQUES: If he weren't talented, he wouldn't write.

MASTER: What?

JACQUES: I said he wouldn't write if he weren't talented.

MASTER (*laughing heartily*): That shows you are nothing but a servant. Do you think everyone who writes has talent? What about that young poet who once came to call on the master of us both?

JACQUES: I don't know any poet.

MASTER: Clearly you know nothing about our master. You are a most uneducated servant.

(*Enter the* INNKEEPER. *She goes up to* JACQUES *and his* MASTER *and bows to them.*)

INNKEEPER: Welcome, gentlemen.

MASTER: And just where are we welcome, Madame?

INNKEEPER: The Great Stag Inn.

MASTER: I don't believe I've heard the name.

INNKEEPER: Bring me a table! And some chairs! *(Two* WAITERS *run in with a table and chairs and seat* JACQUES *and his* MASTER *at them.)* It was written that you would stop at our inn, where you would eat, drink, sleep, and listen to the tales of the innkeeper, who is known far and wide for her exceptionally big mouth.

MASTER: As if my servant's wasn't big enough!

INNKEEPER: What can I do for you, gentlemen?

MASTER *(surveying the* INNKEEPER *with a greedy eye)*: That's worth thinking about.

INNKEEPER: Don't bother. It was written that what you want is duckling, potatoes, and a bottle of wine. . . . *(She exits.)*

JACQUES: You were about to tell me something about a poet, sir.

MASTER *(still under the charm of the* INNKEEPER*)*: Poet?

JACQUES: The young poet who once paid a visit to the master of us both . . .

MASTER: Oh, yes. Well, one day a young poet came to call on the master who invented us. He was constantly being pestered by poets. There's always a surplus of young poets. They increase at the rate of approximately four hundred thousand a year. In France alone. It's even worse in less cultivated countries!

JACQUES: What do people do with them? Drown them?

MASTER: They used to. In the good old days, in Sparta. Back then, poets were tossed from a high rock into the sea the moment they were born. But in our enlightened century we let all sorts live out their days.

*(The* INNKEEPER *brings back a bottle of wine and fills their glasses.)*

INNKEEPER: How do you like it?

MASTER *(tasting it)*: Excellent! Leave the bottle. *(The* INN-KEEPER *exits.)* Now then, one day a young poet turned up at our master's with a sheet of paper. "What a surprise," said our master, "these are poems!" "Yes, Master, poems from my own pen," said the poet, "and I beg you to tell me the truth about them, nothing but the truth." "And are you not afraid of the truth?" said our master. "No," the poet answered in a quavering voice. And our master said to him: "My friend, not only have you shown me that your poems are not worth their weight in shit; your work will never be any better!" "I'm sorry to hear that," said the young poet. "It means I shall have to write bad poetry all my life." To which our master replied, "Let me warn you, young man. Neither gods nor men nor signposts forgive mediocrity in a poet!" "I understand, master," said the poet, "but I can't help myself. It's a compulsion."

JACQUES: A what?

MASTER: A compulsion. "I have a tremendous compulsion to write bad verse." "Let me warn you again of the consequences!" our master exclaimed, but the young poet replied, "You are the great Diderot, I am a bad poet. But we bad poets are the most numerous; we'll always be in the majority! All of mankind consists of bad poets! And the public—its mind, its taste, its sensibility—is nothing but a crowd of bad poets! Why do you think that bad poets offend other bad poets? The bad poets who make up mankind are crazy about bad verse! Indeed, it is just because I write bad verse that I shall one day be in the pantheon of great poets!"

JACQUES: Is that what the young poet said to our master?

MASTER: His very words.

JACQUES: They're not without a certain truth.

MASTER: Certainly not. And that gives me a blasphemous thought.

JACQUES: I know what it is.

MASTER: You do?

JACQUES: I do.

MASTER: Out with it, then.

JACQUES: No, you had it first.

MASTER: We had it simultaneously. Don't lie, now.

JACQUES: I had it after you.

MASTER: All right then. What is it? Come now! Out with it!

JACQUES: You suddenly wondered whether *our* master wasn't a bad poet too.

MASTER: And who's to say he wasn't?

JACQUES: Do you think we'd be better if we'd been invented by somebody else?

MASTER *(thoughtfully)*: It depends. If we'd sprung from the pen of a truly great writer, a genius . . . certainly.

JACQUES *(sadly, after a pause)*: It's sad, you know?

MASTER: What's sad?

JACQUES: That you have such a low opinion of your creator.

MASTER *(looking at* JACQUES*)*: I judge the creator by his work.

JACQUES: We should love the master who made us what we are. We'd be much happier if we loved him. More serene and self-confident. But you, you want a better creator. To be quite frank, Master, I call that blasphemy.

INNKEEPER *(entering with food on a tray)*: Your duckling, gentlemen . . . And when you're finished eating, I'll tell you the story of Madame de La Pommeraye.

JACQUES *(annoyed)*: When we're finished eating, *I'm* going to tell you about how I fell in love!

INNKEEPER: Your master will decide who speaks first.

MASTER: No, no! I refuse! It all depends on what is written on high!

INNKEEPER: What is written on high is that it's my turn to speak.

# ACT TWO

## *Scene 1*

*The setting is the same: the stage is entirely empty except for the downstage table at which* JACQUES *and his* MASTER *are sitting as they come to the end of their supper.*

JACQUES: It all began with the loss of my virginity. I went out and got drunk, my father gave me a beating, a regiment was passing through . . .

INNKEEPER *(entering)*: Was it good?

MASTER: Delicious!

JACQUES: Excellent!

INNKEEPER: Another bottle?

MASTER: Why not?

INNKEEPER *(calling offstage)*: Another bottle! . . . *(To* JACQUES *and his* MASTER.) I promised to tell the gentlemen the story of Madame de La Pommeraye to round off their fine supper. . . .

JACQUES: Damn it all, Madame Innkeeper! I'm telling about how I fell in love!

INNKEEPER: Men are quick to fall in love and just as quick to throw you over. Nothing new about that. Now *I'm* going to tell you a story of how they get their comeuppance.

JACQUES: You have a big mouth, Madame Innkeeper, and eighteen thousand barrels of words in your gullet, and you're always on the lookout for an unfortunate ear to spill them in!

INNKEEPER: You have a perfect lout for a servant, Monsieur. He thinks he's a wit and dares to keep interrupting a lady.

MASTER *(reprovingly)*: Do stop putting yourself forward, Jacques. . . .

INNKEEPER: Now then, there once was a marquis by the name of Des Arcis. An odd bird and incorrigible skirt-chaser. In short, a fine fellow. Only he had no respect for women.

JACQUES: For good reason.

INNKEEPER: You're interrupting, Monsieur Jacques!

JACQUES: I'm not speaking to you, Madame Keeper of the Great Stag Inn.

INNKEEPER: In any case, the Marquis got wind of a certain Marquise de La Pommeraye, a widow of good manners and birth, of wealth and dignity. After duly taxing the Marquis's time and energy, she succumbed at last and bestowed her favors on him. In a few years, however, his interest began to wane. You know what I mean, gentlemen. First he suggested that they spend more time in society. Then that she entertain more. Soon he failed to appear at her receptions. He always had something urgent to attend to. When he did come to see her, he would scarcely speak, would stretch out in an armchair, pick up a book, toss it aside, play with her dog, and then fall asleep in her presence. But Madame de La Pommeraye still loved him, and suffered dreadfully, until one day, proud woman that she was, she flew into a rage and determined to put an end to it.

# Scene 2

*During the speech of the* INNKEEPER, *the* MARQUIS *enters upstage on the platform, carrying a chair. He sets it down, then drops into it, lazily and with an air of bliss.*

INNKEEPER *(turning to the* MARQUIS*)*: My dear friend . . .

OFFSTAGE VOICE: Madame Innkeeper!

INNKEEPER *(calling offstage)*: What is it?

OFFSTAGE VOICE: The key to the pantry!

INNKEEPER: It's hanging on the hook. . . . *(To the* MARQUIS.*)* You're dreaming, my friend. . . . *(She mounts the platform and walks over to the* MARQUIS.*)*

MARQUIS: As are you, Marquise.

INNKEEPER: True, and rather sad dreams at that.

MARQUIS: What's ailing you, Marquise?

INNKEEPER: Oh, nothing.

MARQUIS *(yawning)*: Not so! Come now, Marquise, do tell me. If nothing else, it'll dispel our boredom.

INNKEEPER: So you're bored, are you?

MARQUIS: No, no! . . . It's just that there are days . . . when . . .

INNKEEPER: . . . when we are bored together.

MARQUIS: No! It's not that, my dear. . . . But there are days . . . Heaven only knows why . . .

INNKEEPER: There's something I've long been meaning to tell you, my friend. I only fear it will grieve you.

MARQUIS: You? Grieve me?

INNKEEPER: Heaven only knows I'm not at fault in the matter.

OFFSTAGE VOICE: Madame Innkeeper!

INNKEEPER *(calling offstage)*: Haven't I told you to stop bothering me? Ask my husband!

OFFSTAGE VOICE: He's not here!

INNKEEPER: Well, what the hell is it this time?

OFFSTAGE VOICE: The straw merchant.

INNKEEPER: Pay him and chuck him out. . . . *(To the MAR-QUIS.)* Yes, Marquis, it happened before I was even aware of it, and I myself am devastated. Every night I ask myself, "Is the Marquis any less worthy of my love? Have I any reason to reproach him? Has he been unfaithful? No! Then why has my heart changed when his remains constant? I no longer feel alarmed when he's late nor sweetly moved when at last he appears."

MARQUIS *(joyfully)*: Really!

INNKEEPER *(covering her eyes with her hands)*: Oh, Marquis! Spare me your reproaches. . . . Or rather, no. Spare me not. I deserve them. . . . Should I have concealed my feelings? I'm the one who has changed, not you. That is why I respect you more than ever. I'll not lie to myself. Love has abandoned my heart. It is a terrible discovery, terrible but true.

MARQUIS *(falling at her feet with joy)*: You charming creature, you! You are the most charming woman on earth! How happy you have made me! Your sincerity puts me to shame. You tower above me! I am nothing next to you! For the tale your heart tells is word for word the tale my heart would tell, had I but the courage to speak.

INNKEEPER: Is that true?

MARQUIS: Nothing could be truer. Now the only thing left for us to do is rejoice that we've both lost, at the very same time, the fragile and deceptive sentiment uniting us.

INNKEEPER: Quite. It is a great misfortune when one continues to love after the other no longer does.

MARQUIS: Never have you appeared more lovely to me than in this moment, and if experience had not made a prudent man of me, I should go so far as to say that I love you more than ever.

INNKEEPER: But, Marquis, what do we do now?

MARQUIS: We have never deceived each other nor spoken falsely. You have a right to my deepest respect; I trust I have not entirely lost yours. We shall be the best of friends. We shall assist each other in our amorous intrigues! And who knows what may happen one day. . . .

JACQUES: Good God, who does know?

MARQUIS: Perhaps . . .

OFFSTAGE VOICE: Where's my wife gone to?

INNKEEPER *(calling offstage, annoyed)*: What do you want?

OFFSTAGE VOICE: Nothing!

INNKEEPER *(to* JACQUES *and his* MASTER*)*: It's enough to drive you crazy, gentlemen! Wouldn't you know he'd call me just when things seem to have settled down in this godforsaken hole, just when everyone's asleep. Now he's made me lose the thread, the clumsy oaf. . . . *(She steps down from the platform.)* Gentlemen, I am truly to be pitied. . . .

# Scene 3

MASTER: And I am perfectly willing to pity you, Madame. *(He gives her a slap on the behind.)* But I must congratulate you as well, for you are an excellent storyteller. I've just had an odd thought. What if instead of the clumsy oaf, as you've just called your husband, you were married to Monsieur Jacques here? What I mean is, what would a husband who never stops jabbering do with a wife who never closes her mouth?

JACQUES: Exactly what my grandmother and grandfather did with me all the years I lived with them. They were very strict. They'd get up, get dressed, get to work; then eat and go back to work. In the evening, Grandmother did her sewing and Grandfather read the Bible. Nobody said a word all day.

MASTER: And you? What did you do?

JACQUES: I ran back and forth in the room with a gag in my mouth!

INNKEEPER: A gag?

JACQUES: Grandfather liked his quiet. So I spent the first twelve years of my life gagged. . . .

INNKEEPER *(calling offstage)*: Jean!

OFFSTAGE VOICE: What is it?

INNKEEPER: Two more bottles! But not the ones we serve the customers. Way in the back, behind the firewood!

OFFSTAGE VOICE: Right!

INNKEEPER: Monsieur Jacques, I've changed my mind about you. You're actually quite a touching man. The moment I pictured you with that gag in your mouth, dying to talk, I felt a great love for you well up inside me. What do you say? . . . Let's make peace. *(They embrace.)*

*(A waiter enters and places two bottles on the table. He opens them and fills three glasses.)*

INNKEEPER: Gentlemen, you'll never drink a better wine!

JACQUES: You must have been a devilishly beautiful woman, Madame Innkeeper!

MASTER: You lout! She *is* a devilishly beautiful woman!

INNKEEPER: Oh, I'm not what I used to be. You should have seen me in my prime! But that's neither here nor there. . . . Back to Madame de La Pommeraye . . .

JACQUES *(raising his glass)*: But first, to every man whose head you've turned!

INNKEEPER: With pleasure. *(They clink glasses and drink.)* And now . . . Madame de La Pommeraye.

JACQUES: But first, let's drink to Monsieur le Marquis. I'm worried about him.

INNKEEPER: And well you might be.

*(They clink glasses and drink.)*

# Scene 4

*During the last lines of the preceding scene,* MOTHER *and* DAUGHTER *have entered and mounted the platform upstage.*

INNKEEPER: Can you imagine her fury? Telling the Marquis she no longer loves him and watching him jump for joy! Gentlemen, she had her pride! *(She turns toward the* MOTHER *and* DAUGHTER.) So she sought out these two creatures. Women she had known long before. A mother and daughter. They had come to Paris for a lawsuit, and having lost it, were ruined. The mother was reduced to running a small casino.

MOTHER *(from the platform)*: Necessity knows no law. I did everything possible to place my daughter at the Opéra. Is it my fault the silly goose has a rasp for a voice?

INNKEEPER: The gentlemen who frequented the casino came to gamble and dine, but more often than not, one or two would stay on and spend the night with mother or daughter. Which makes the two of them . . .

JACQUES: Which makes the two of them . . . But, let's drink their health all the same. Like your wine, they go down nicely. (JACQUES *raises his glass. All three clink glasses and drink.)*

MOTHER *(to the* INNKEEPER*)*: I shall be frank, Madame la Marquise. Our profession is a delicate one and quite dangerous.

INNKEEPER *(mounting the platform and going up to the* MOTHER *and* DAUGHTER*)*: I hope you're not too well known in the profession.

MOTHER: Fortunately not. At least I don't believe so. Our . . . establishment . . . is located in the Rue de Hambourg . . . on the outskirts of town. . . .

INNKEEPER: I presume you have no desire to persist in your profession and would not be averse to bettering your lot if I saw fit to help you.

MOTHER *(with gratitude)*: Oh, Madame la Marquise!

INNKEEPER: Then you must do everything I say.

MOTHER: You may count on us.

INNKEEPER: Very well, then. Return home. Sell all your furniture and any clothes that are the least bit ostentatious.

JACQUES *(raising his glass)*: To the health of Mademoiselle! No doubt that melancholy air of hers comes from changing masters every night.

INNKEEPER *(to* JACQUES *from the platform)*: Don't mock her, Monsieur. If only you knew how nauseating it can be! *(To the two women.)* I shall find you some rooms and have them furnished as soberly as possible. You are to leave them only to go to church. You are to walk with your eyes to the ground and never go off anywhere on your own. You are to speak only of God. I shall of course refrain from visiting you. I am unworthy . . . to associate with women as devout as you. . . . And now, do as I say! *(The two women exit.)*

MASTER: That woman gives me the shudders.

INNKEEPER *(to* MASTER *from the platform)*: And you don't even know her yet.

# *Scene 5*

*The* MARQUIS *has entered from the other side of the stage. He goes up to the* INNKEEPER *and touches her arm lightly. Surprised, she turns to face him.*

INNKEEPER: Oh, Marquis! How glad I am to see you! What news do you bring of your intrigues? Of all your tender little girls?

*(The* MARQUIS *takes her by the arm and strolls back and*

*forth along the platform with her, leaning over and whispering his response in her ear.)*

MASTER: Look at them, Jacques! He's telling her everything, the blind pig!

INNKEEPER: I do admire you! *(The* MARQUIS *whispers something else in her ear.)* Still the successful womanizer!

MARQUIS: Well, and have *you* nothing to confide? *(The* INNKEEPER *shakes her head.)* What about that runt of a count, that dwarf who was always after you. . . ?

INNKEEPER: I no longer see him.

MARQUIS: Well, well! What made you give him up?

INNKEEPER: I didn't care for him.

MARQUIS: Didn't care for him? The most adorable of dwarfs? Or is it that you're still in love with me?

INNKEEPER: And if I am. . . ?

MARQUIS: So you're counting on my return and hoping to reap the benefits of your spotless conduct!

INNKEEPER: Does that frighten you?

MARQUIS: You're a dangerous woman!

*(Continuing their stroll, the* MARQUIS *and the* INNKEEPER *notice two women coming from the opposite direction; they are the* MOTHER *and* DAUGHTER.*)*

INNKEEPER *(feigning surprise)*: Goodness! Can it be? *(She lets go of the* MARQUIS's *arm and goes up to the two women.)* Is it you, Madame?

MOTHER: Yes, it is I.

INNKEEPER: How are you? What's become of you after all these years?

MOTHER: You know of our misfortunes. We lead a modest and secluded existence.

INNKEEPER: You do well to shun society, but why shun me? . . .

DAUGHTER: I have often spoken to Mother of you, Madame, but she always says, "Madame de La Pommeraye? Surely she has forgotten us."

INNKEEPER: How unjust! I'm delighted to see you. This is Monsieur le Marquis des Arcis. He's a friend of mine. You may speak freely in his presence. My, how Mademoiselle has grown!

*(All four continue their stroll together.)*

MASTER: You know, Jacques, I like that innkeeper. Mark my words, she wasn't born at any inn. She's of a higher station. I have a sense for such things.

INNKEEPER: Indeed! You've blossomed into a beauty.

MASTER: Say what you like. She's a noble female.

MARQUIS *(to the two women)*: Stay awhile! Please! Don't go!

MOTHER *(timidly)*: No, no. We shall be late for vespers. . . . Come along, my dear. *(They bow and exit.)*

MARQUIS: Heavens, Marquise! Who are those women?

INNKEEPER: The happiest creatures I know. Did you notice how calm they were, how serene? There's much to be said for a life of seclusion.

MARQUIS: It would cause me great remorse, Marquise, to learn that our separation has led you to such lamentable extremes.

INNKEEPER: Would you rather I opened my door again to the count?

MARQUIS: The runt? Most certainly.

INNKEEPER: Is that what you advise me to do?

MARQUIS: Without the slightest hesitation.

INNKEEPER (*stepping down from the platform; to* JACQUES *and his* MASTER): Do you hear that? (*She picks up her glass from the table and takes a drink. Then she sits on the edge of the platform. The* MARQUIS *sits beside her.*) How old she makes me feel! When I first saw her, she hardly came up to my waist.

MARQUIS: You mean that woman's daughter?

INNKEEPER: Yes. I feel like a wilted rose next to one in bloom. Did you notice her?

MARQUIS: Obviously.

INNKEEPER: What do you think of her?

MARQUIS: She's like a Raphael madonna.

INNKEEPER: Those eyes!

MARQUIS: That voice!

INNKEEPER: That skin!

MARQUIS: That walk!

INNKEEPER: That smile!

JACQUES: Good Lord! If you go on like this, Marquis, you're done for!

INNKEEPER (*to* JACQUES): Right you are. He's done for. (*She stands, picks up her glass, and takes a drink.*)

MARQUIS: That body! (*With these words, he stands and exits, describing a semicircle on the platform as he goes.*)

INNKEEPER (*to* JACQUES *and his* MASTER): He's swallowed the bait.

JACQUES: Madame Innkeeper, she's a monster, your Marquise.

INNKEEPER: And the Marquis? He shouldn't have fallen out of love with her!

JACQUES: I see, Madame, that you don't know the pretty little fable of the Knife and the Sheath.

MASTER: Nor do I. You've never told it to me!

## Scene 6

*The* MARQUIS *retraces his semicircle downstage in the direction of the* INNKEEPER *and begins to speak to her in a supplicatory voice.*

MARQUIS: Tell me, Marquise, have you met your friends lately?

INNKEEPER *(to* JACQUES *and his* MASTER*)*: You see? He's caught.

MARQUIS: It's not right of you! They're so poor, and you never invite them to dine.

INNKEEPER: Ah, I do. But in vain. And no wonder. If word got round that they were seeing me, people would say Madame de La Pommeraye was their patron and they would forfeit their charity.

MARQUIS: What! They live on charity?

INNKEEPER: Yes, charity from their parish.

MARQUIS: They're your friends, and they live on charity?

INNKEEPER: Ah, Marquis. We who move in society are ill-equipped to appreciate the sensitivity of such God-fearing souls. They won't accept aid indiscriminately. It must come from pure, unsullied hands.

MARQUIS: Do you know that I was tempted to visit them?

INNKEEPER: A visit from you could be their downfall. With that girl's charms, it wouldn't take long before tongues began to wag!

MARQUIS *(with a sigh)*: How cruel . . .

INNKEEPER *(maliciously)*: Cruel is the word.

MARQUIS: You mock me, Marquise.

INNKEEPER: I'm merely trying to save you grief. You're letting yourself in for great agony, Marquis! Don't confuse this girl with the women you've known! She will not be tempted. You'll never have your way with her!

*(Crushed, the* MARQUIS *withdraws upstage in a semicircle.)*

JACQUES: How spiteful she is, your Marquise.

INNKEEPER *(to* JACQUES*)*: Don't try to defend your sex, Monsieur Jacques. Have you forgotten so soon how Madame de La Pommeraye loved the Marquis? Why, she's smitten with him even now. His every word is like a dagger in her heart! Can't you see the inferno they both have ahead of them?

*(The* MARQUIS *returns to the* INNKEEPER *in a semicircle. She looks up at him.)*

INNKEEPER: Heavens! You look dreadful!

MARQUIS *(walking back and forth across the platform)*: I'm haunted. I can't stand it. Can't sleep. Can't eat. For weeks I drank like a fish. Then I turned pious like a monk to catch a glimpse of her in church. . . . Marquise! Find a way for me to see her again! *(The* INNKEEPER *heaves a sigh.)* You're my only friend!

INNKEEPER: I should be only too glad to help you, Marquis, but the situation is delicate. She must never think I'm in collusion with you. . . .

MARQUIS: I beg of you!

INNKEEPER *(imitating him)*: I beg of you! . . . What do I care if you're in love or not! Why should I complicate my life? You'll have to manage on your own!

MARQUIS: I implore you! Abandon me now and I am lost. Do it for their sake if not for mine! I warn you, I'm desperate! I'll break down their door, stop at nothing!

INNKEEPER: So be it. . . . As you like. But at least give me time to make the necessary preparations. . . .

*(SERVANTS set chairs around the table upstage as the MARQUIS exits.)*

# *Scene 7*

INNKEEPER *(to the MOTHER and DAUGHTER, who enter upstage)*: Come in, come in. Sit here with me at the table, and we'll begin. *(They take their seats at the upstage table. There are now two tables on the stage: one at the foot of the platform, downstage, where JACQUES and his MASTER are sitting, and one on the platform, upstage.)* When the Marquis arrives, we'll all feign surprise. Remember to stay in character.

JACQUES *(calling up to the INNKEEPER)*: Madame Innkeeper, she's a beast, that woman!

INNKEEPER *(calling down to JACQUES)*: And the Marquis, Monsieur Jacques, is he an angel?

JACQUES: But no one is asking him to be an angel. Or do you think man has no choice but to be angel or beast? You'd be wiser if you knew the fable of the Knife and the Sheath.

MARQUIS (*approaching the women with pretended surprise*): Oh . . . I hope I am not disturbing you. . . .

INNKEEPER (*also surprised*): In truth . . . we weren't expecting you, Monsieur le Marquis. . . .

MASTER: What actors!

INNKEEPER: But since you're here, please join us for dinner.

(*The* MARQUIS *kisses the ladies' hands and takes a seat.*)

JACQUES: This promises to be dull. Let me tell you the fable of the Knife and the Sheath.

MARQUIS (*entering into the ladies' discussion*): I quite agree with you. What are the pleasures of life? Ashes and dust. Can you guess what man I admire most?

JACQUES: Don't listen to him, sir.

MARQUIS: You can't, can you? Well, it's Saint Simeon Stylites, my patron saint.

JACQUES: The fable of the Knife and the Sheath is the moral of all morals and the foundation of all knowledge.

MARQUIS: Just think, dear ladies! Saint Simeon spent forty years of his life praying to God atop a pillar forty meters high.

JACQUES: Listen to me. One day the Knife and the Sheath had a quarrel. "Sheath, darling," said the Knife, "I wish you weren't such a slut, giving refuge every day to new knives." To which the Sheath replied, "Knife, darling, I wish you weren't such a lecher, taking refuge every day in new sheaths."

MARQUIS: Just think, dear ladies, forty years of his life on a pillar forty meters high!

JACQUES: The quarrel broke out while they were at dinner, and a guest sitting between them spoke up. "Dear Sheath," he said, "dear Knife, you do no wrong in changing knives and sheaths. You did commit a fatal error, though, the day you promised not to change. For do you not yet see, Friend Knife, that God made you to slip into many sheaths?"

DAUGHTER: Tell me, was the column really forty meters high?

JACQUES: "And you, Friend Sheath, do you not see that God made you to accommodate many knives?"

*(The* MASTER *has been listening to* JACQUES *without paying attention to the platform. After these words he laughs.)*

MARQUIS *(with a lover's tenderness)*: Yes, my child. Forty meters high.

DAUGHTER: Didn't Saint Simeon suffer from vertigo?

MARQUIS: No, he did not. And do you know why, my dear child?

DAUGHTER: No.

MARQUIS: Because he never once looked down from the top of his pillar. He never stopped looking upward, to God. And he who looks upward is forever free of vertigo.

THE LADIES *(astonished)*: How true!

MASTER: Jacques!

JACQUES: Yes?

MARQUIS *(taking leave of the ladies)*: It has been a great honor. . . . *(He exits.)*

MASTER *(amused)*: Your fable is immoral, Jacques, and I reject and renounce it, declare it null and void.

JACQUES: But you enjoyed it!

MASTER: That's beside the point! Who wouldn't? Of course I enjoyed it!

*(The* SERVANTS *remove the table and chairs upstage.* JACQUES *and his* MASTER *turn back to watch the platform. The* MARQUIS *goes up to the* INNKEEPER.*)*

# *Scene 8*

INNKEEPER: Tell me now, Marquis: Is there another woman in all of France who would do for you what I am doing?

MARQUIS *(kneeling before her)*: You are my one true friend. . . .

INNKEEPER: Let's change the subject. What does your heart tell you?

MARQUIS: I'll have that girl or perish.

INNKEEPER: I'd be very glad to save your life.

MARQUIS: I know it will upset you, but I must confess: I sent them a letter. And a jewel box filled with gems. But they sent both of them back.

INNKEEPER *(sternly)*: Love is corrupting you, Marquis. What have those two poor women done to you to make you so intent on defiling them? Do you really think that virtue can be bought with a handful of gems?

MARQUIS *(still on his knees)*: Forgive me.

INNKEEPER: I warned you. But you're incorrigible.

MARQUIS: Dear friend, I want to make one last try. I'm going to give them one of my houses in town and another in the country. I'm going to give them half of everything I possess.

INNKEEPER: As you wish . . . But honor has no price. I know these women.

*(She walks away from the* MARQUIS, *leaving him on his knees, and toward the* MOTHER, *who comes up to her from the other side of the platform and kneels before her.)*

MOTHER: Madame la Marquise, don't forbid us to accept his offer! So great a fortune! So great an estate! So great an honor!

INNKEEPER *(to the* MOTHER, *still on her knees)*: Do you imagine I've done what I've done for the sake of your happiness? You shall go and refuse the Marquis's offer at once.

JACQUES: What is she after now, that woman?

INNKEEPER *(to* JACQUES*)*: Whatever it may be, it's not likely to further the interests of the two women. They're nothing to her, Monsieur Jacques! *(To the* MOTHER.*)* Either you do as I say or I send you straight back to your brothel! *(She turns away from her and back toward the* MARQUIS, *who is still on his knees. The* MOTHER *rises and exits slowly.)*

MARQUIS: Dear friend, how right you were. They've refused. I'm at my wit's end. What shall I do? Ah, Marquise, do you know what I've decided? I've decided to marry her.

INNKEEPER *(feigning surprise)*: A serious move, Marquis. It deserves careful thought.

MARQUIS: To what end, Marquise? I can never be more unhappy than I am at present.

INNKEEPER: Don't be rash, Marquis. A hasty decision could ruin your entire life.... *(Pretending to think.)* Though they *are* virtuous, these women. Their hearts are pure as crystal ... Perhaps you're right. Poverty is no crime.

MARQUIS: Go and see them, I beg of you, and tell them of my intentions.

*(The INNKEEPER turns to the MARQUIS and offers him her hand. He rises, and the two stand face to face. The MARQUIS smiles.)*

INNKEEPER: Very well, then. I promise to do so.

MARQUIS: Thank you.

INNKEEPER: What wouldn't I do for you?

MARQUIS *(in a rush of euphoria)*: Then why not, as my only true friend, why not join me and take a husband?

INNKEEPER: Have you someone in mind, Marquis?

MARQUIS: Why, the little count.

INNKEEPER: The dwarf?

MARQUIS: He's wealthy, witty ...

INNKEEPER: And who will vouch for his fidelity? You, perhaps?

MARQUIS: One can easily do without fidelity in a husband.

INNKEEPER: No, no, not I. I'd be offended. And then, I'm vindictive.

MARQUIS: If you're vindictive, we'll have our revenge together. Yes, not a bad idea! Do you know what? We'll rent a town house and be a happy foursome.

INNKEEPER: Yes, not a bad idea.

MARQUIS: And if your dwarf gets on your nerves, we'll drop him in the flower vase on your bed table.

INNKEEPER: Your proposition is highly attractive, but I will not marry. The only man who could ever be my husband . . .

MARQUIS: Is the Marquis des Arcis?

INNKEEPER: I can admit it to you now fearlessly.

MARQUIS: And why did you say nothing before?

INNKEEPER: By the look of things, I was right not to. The woman you've chosen is much more suited to you.

*(The* DAUGHTER *appears upstage in a white wedding gown and advances slowly. The* MARQUIS *sees her and moves toward her as if in a trance.)*

MARQUIS: Marquise, I'll be grateful to you to the grave. . . . *(When he reaches the* DAUGHTER, *they freeze in a long embrace.)*

# Scene 9

*While the* MARQUIS *and the* DAUGHTER *embrace, the* INNKEEPER *moves backward to the other end of the platform without taking her eyes off the* MARQUIS. *At last she calls out to him.*

INNKEEPER: Marquis! *(The* MARQUIS *fails to react. He is lost in his embrace.)* Marquis! *(The* MARQUIS *turns his head slightly.)* Were you satisfied with your wedding night?

JACQUES: Good God! And how!

INNKEEPER: I'm so glad. Now listen carefully. Once you had an honorable woman, but you were unable to hold on to her. I was that woman. *(JACQUES begins to laugh.)* I have avenged myself by inducing you to marry the sort of woman you deserve. Pay a visit to the Rue de Hambourg, and you'll learn how your wife earned her living! Your wife and your mother-in-law! *(She bursts into a devilish laugh.)*

*(The DAUGHTER throws herself at the MARQUIS's feet.)*

MARQUIS: You vile creature, you! . . .

DAUGHTER *(at the MARQUIS's feet)*: Trample me, Monsieur, crush me! . . .

MARQUIS: Out, you vile creature! . . .

DAUGHTER: Do as you will with me! . . .

INNKEEPER: Quickly, Marquis! To the Rue de Hambourg! And while you're there, have a plaque put up, a plaque that says: "The Marquise des Arcis slept here—with one and all." *(She laughs her devilish laugh again.)*

DAUGHTER *(at the MARQUIS's feet)*: Have pity on me, Monsieur! . . .

*(As the MARQUIS kicks her away, she grabs hold of his leg, but he shakes her loose and exits. The DAUGHTER remains on the ground.)*

JACQUES: Just a minute, Madame Innkeeper! That can't be the end of the story!

INNKEEPER: Of course it can. And don't you add one jot to it!

*(JACQUES leaps up on the platform and takes the place recently vacated by the MARQUIS. The DAUGHTER grabs hold of his leg.)*

DAUGHTER: Monsieur le Marquis, I implore you! Grant me at least the hope that you can forgive me!

JACQUES: Stand up.

DAUGHTER *(on the ground, clutching his knees)*: Do with me as you see fit! I'll submit to anything!

JACQUES *(in a sincere voice, moved)*: Please stand up, Madame . . . *(The* DAUGHTER *does not dare stand.)* So many honorable girls turn into dishonorable women. Why not reverse the process for once? *(Tenderly.)* I firmly believe that debauchery has never tainted, no, never even touched you. Stand up. Don't you hear me? I've forgiven you. Even in the depths of disgrace I never ceased to think of you as my wife. Be honorable, be faithful, be happy, and make me happy. I ask nothing more of you. Stand up, dear wife. Madame la Marquise, stand up! Stand up, Madame des Arcis!

*(The* DAUGHTER *picks herself up, puts her arms around* JACQUES, *and kisses him passionately.)*

INNKEEPER *(calling out from the other side of the platform)*: She's a whore, Marquis!

JACQUES: Hold your tongue, Madame de La Pommeraye! *(To the* DAUGHTER.*)* I've forgiven you and want you to know I have no regrets. As for that woman *(he nods in the . direction of the* INNKEEPER*)*, not only has she failed to avenge herself; she has done me an immense service. Are you not younger than she, more beautiful, and infinitely more devoted? And now, off to the country, where we're going to have years of happiness. *(He leads her across the platform, then stops and turns to the* INNKEEPER, *dropping the role of* MARQUIS.*)* And I must tell you, Madame Innkeeper, they were very happy years. Because nothing on earth is certain, and the meaning of things changes as the wind blows. And the wind blows constantly, whether you know it or not. And the wind blows, and joy turns to sorrow, revenge to reward, and a loose woman becomes a faithful wife with whom none can compare. . . .

# *Scene 10*

*Toward the end of* Jacques's *speech, the* Innkeeper *comes down from the platform and takes a seat at the table where* Jacques's Master *is sitting. The* Master *puts his arm around her waist and drinks with her.*

Master: Jacques, I don't like the way you've finished off the story! That girl doesn't deserve to be a marquise! She bears a striking resemblance to Agathe! A fine pair of cheats, those two.

Jacques: You're mistaken, sir!

Master: What? I? Mistaken?

Jacques: Badly mistaken.

Master: Since when has a Jacques the right to tell his master whether he's mistaken or not?

*(Leaving the* Daughter, *who exits during the following dialogue,* Jacques *leaps down from the platform.)*

Jacques: I'm not merely "a Jacques." You've even been known to call me your friend.

Master *(fondling the* Innkeeper*)*: When I call you my friend, you're my friend. When I call you "a Jacques," you're "a Jacques." Because on high, and you know where that is, on high, as your captain used to say, on high it is written that I am your master. And I command you to retract your version of the story's conclusion, which displeases not only me but also Madame de La Pommeraye, whom I greatly respect *(he kisses the* INNKEEPER*)* as a woman of nobility with a magnificent ass. . . .

JACQUES: Do you really believe, Master, that Jacques would retract a story he told?

MASTER: If his master so wills it, Jacques will retract his story!

JACQUES: That'll be the day, sir!

MASTER *(still fondling the* INNKEEPER*)*: If Jacques persists in answering his master back, his master will send Jacques to the shed to sleep among the goats!

JACQUES: Well, I won't go!

MASTER *(kissing the* INNKEEPER*)*: Yes you will.

JACQUES: No I won't.

MASTER *(loudly)*: Yes you will!

INNKEEPER: Would you do a favor for a lady you've just kissed, Monsieur?

MASTER: Anything her heart desires.

INNKEEPER: Then do stop quarreling with your servant. I realize he's insolent, but isn't that precisely what you need in a servant? It is written on high that the two of you will be unable to do without each other.

MASTER *(to* JACQUES*)*: Do you hear that, servant? Madame de La Pommeraye says I'll never be rid of you.

JACQUES: Oh, yes you will be rid of me, Master, because I'm off to spend the night with the goats.

MASTER *(standing up)*: No you're not!

JACQUES: Yes I am! *(He begins to exit slowly.)*

MASTER: No you're not!

JACQUES: Yes I am!

MASTER: Jacques! *(JACQUES continues to exit, but more slowly.)* Jacques, my boy! *(JACQUES continues to exit, but very slowly.)* Jacques, dear boy . . . *(The MASTER runs after him and grabs him by the arm.)* Well, did you hear that? What would I do without you?

JACQUES: All right, then. But to prevent future disputes, let's lay down our principles once and for all.

MASTER: Agreed.

JACQUES: So! Whereas it is written on high that I am indispensable to you, I shall exploit you whenever the opportunity arises.

MASTER: That's not written on high!

JACQUES: All of that was set down the moment our master invented us. It was he who decided that you would have appearance and I would have substance. That you would give the orders and I choose among them. That you would have power and I influence.

MASTER: If that's the case, then we're switching places.

JACQUES: And where would that get you? You'd lose appearance without gaining substance. You'd lose power without gaining influence. Stay as you are, sir. And if you're a good master and do as I say, I promise not to be hard on you.

INNKEEPER: Amen. But now that night has fallen, it is written on high that we have drunk our fill and must go to bed.

# ACT THREE

## *Scene 1*

*The stage is completely bare except for* JACQUES *and his* MASTER.

MASTER: Tell me, where are our horses?

JACQUES: No more silly questions, sir.

MASTER: It's utter nonsense! A Frenchman traveling through France on foot! Do you know who it is who dared rewrite our story?

JACQUES: An imbecile, sir. But now that our story is rewritten, we can't make any changes in it.

MASTER: Death to all who dare rewrite what has been written! Impale them and roast them over a slow fire! Castrate them and cut off their ears! My feet hurt.

JACQUES: Rewriters are never burnt, sir. Everybody believes them.

MASTER: You mean they'll believe the one who rewrote our story? They won't bother to read the original book to find out what we're really like?

JACQUES: Our story, sir, isn't the only thing that's been rewritten. Everything that's ever happened here below has been rewritten hundreds of times, and no one ever dreams of finding out what really happened. The history of mankind has been rewritten so often that people don't know who they are anymore.

MASTER: Why, that's appalling! Then they *(indicating the audience)* will believe we haven't even got any horses and had to trudge through our story like tramps?

JACQUES *(indicating the audience)*: They? They'll believe anything!

MASTER: You're in a bad mood today. We should have stayed on at the Great Stag.

JACQUES: Well, I was perfectly willing.

MASTER: Anyway . . . Mark my words. She wasn't born at any inn.

JACQUES: Where then?

MASTER *(dreamily)*: I don't know. But the way she spoke, the way she carried herself . . .

JACQUES: I do think, sir, that you're falling in love.

MASTER *(shrugging his shoulders)*: If it was written on high . . . *(Pause.)* Which reminds me. You still haven't finished telling me how *you* fell in love.

JACQUES: You shouldn't have given priority yesterday to the story of Madame de La Pommeraye.

MASTER: I let a great lady take precedence yesterday. You'll never understand chivalry. But now that you're alone with me, I give you priority.

JACQUES: Much obliged, sir. Now listen carefully. After I lost my virginity, I went out and got drunk. After I went out and got drunk, my father gave me a beating. After my father gave me a beating, I joined a passing regiment. . . .

MASTER: You're repeating yourself, Jacques!

JACQUES: Me? Repeating myself? Really, sir. There is nothing more shameful than repeating yourself. You shouldn't have said that to me. Now I won't open my mouth till the end of the performance.

MASTER: Please, Jacques. I implore you.

JACQUES: You implore me? Now you're imploring me?

MASTER: Yes.

JACQUES: All right, then. Where was I?

MASTER: Your father had just given you a beating. You joined a passing regiment. You ended up in a hut, where you were taken care of by a big-bottomed beauty. . . . *(He stops suddenly.)* Jacques . . . Listen to me, Jacques. . . . I want you to be frank with me. . . . Completely frank, understand? Is it true that that woman had a big ass, or are you just saying so to make me happy?

JACQUES: Why ask unnecessary questions, sir?

MASTER *(melancholy)*: Her bottom wasn't so big, was it?

JACQUES *(gently)*: Don't ask questions, sir. You know I don't like lying to you.

MASTER *(melancholy)*: So you led me astray, Jacques.

JACQUES: Don't hold it against me.

MASTER *(melancholy)*: Of course not, Jacques, my boy. I know you had my best interests at heart.

JACQUES: Yes, sir. I know how much women with big bottoms mean to you.

MASTER: You're a good man, Jacques. You're a good servant. Servants must be good and must tell their masters what they want to hear. Avoid unnecessary truths, Jacques.

JACQUES: Don't worry, sir. I don't like unnecessary truths. I know of nothing more stupid than an unnecessary truth.

MASTER: For example?

JACQUES: For example, that we are mortal. Or that the world is rotten. As if we had to be told. You know the sort who steps on the stage like a hero and cries, "The world is rotten!" Well, the audience applauds, but Jacques isn't interested, because Jacques knew it two hundred, four hundred, eight hundred years before him, and while he and his sort shout, "The world is rotten!" Jacques prefers to please his master. . .

MASTER: . . . his rotten master . . .

JACQUES: . . . his rotten master, by inventing big-bottomed women of the kind he loves so well . . . .

MASTER: Only I know, I and the one up there, that you are the best servant of all servants who ever served.

JACQUES: So don't ask any questions, don't try to learn the truth. Just listen to me: She had a big bottom. . . . Wait a minute. Which one am I talking about?

MASTER: The one in the hut where they took you in.

JACQUES: Oh, yes. I spent a week in bed there, while the doctors drank up their wine. No wonder my benefactors wanted to get rid of me. Luckily, one of the doctors, a surgeon at the château, had a wife who put in a good word for me, and I went to live with them.

MASTER: So there never was anything between you and the pretty woman from the hut.

JACQUES: No.

MASTER: What a shame. But never mind! Tell me about the doctor's wife, the one who put in the good word for you. What was she like?

JACQUES: Blond.

MASTER: Like Agathe.

JACQUES: Long legs.

MASTER: Like Agathe. And her bottom?

JACQUES *(showing him)*: Like this, sir!

MASTER: Agathe all over. *(With indignation.)* Oh, the slut!

I'd have treated her a good deal worse than the Marquis des Arcis treated that little cheat of his! Or Young Bigre his Justine!

*(SAINT-OUEN has appeared on the platform and is following the conversation between JACQUES and his MASTER with great interest.)*

SAINT-OUEN: And why didn't you?

JACQUES *(to his MASTER)*: Do you hear him mock you? He's a scoundrel, sir. I told you so the first time you mentioned him to me.

MASTER: He's a scoundrel, all right, but for the moment he's done no more than what you did to your friend Bigre.

JACQUES: Yet clearly only he is a scoundrel, not I.

MASTER *(struck by the veracity of JACQUES's remark)*: Why, that's true. You both seduce your best friends' women, yet only he is a scoundrel, and not you. How do you explain that?

JACQUES: I don't know, sir. But I have a feeling that in the depths of that riddle there hides a profound truth.

MASTER: Of course! And I know what it is! The difference between the two of you is not in your deeds but in your souls! You cuckolded your friend Bigre, but then you drowned your sorrows.

JACQUES: I hate to destroy your illusions, but I wasn't drowning my sorrows, I was celebrating. . . .

MASTER: You mean you didn't get drunk out of remorse?

JACQUES: It's shameful, I know, but that's how it is.

MASTER: Jacques, would you do something for me?

JACQUES: For you? Anything you ask.

MASTER: Let's agree that you were drowning your sorrows.

JACQUES: If that is what you wish, sir.

MASTER: That is what I wish.

JACQUES: So be it, sir. I was drowning my sorrows.

MASTER: Thank you. I want to distinguish you as clearly as possible from that scoundrel *(turning toward* SAINT-OUEN, *who is still on the platform),* who, by the way, was not content merely to cuckold me. . . . *(He mounts the platform.)*

# Scene 2

SAINT-OUEN: Dear friend! The time has come to think of revenge! And since she has harmed us both, the wretch, I propose we avenge ourselves together!

JACQUES: Yes, I remember. That's where we left off. Well, sir! What did you tell the rat?

MASTER *(looking at* JACQUES *from the platform, pathetically)*: What did I tell him? Look at me, Jacques. Look at me, my boy. Look at me and weep at my fate! *(To* SAINT-OUEN.*)* Listen, Saint-Ouen, I'm willing to put your betrayal behind me on one condition.

JACQUES: Good for you, Master! Don't let him push you around!

SAINT-OUEN: Anything you say. Shall I jump out of the window? *(The* MASTER *smiles and does not respond.)* Hang myself? *(The* MASTER *does not respond.)* Drown myself? *(The* MASTER *does not respond.)* Plunge a knife into my breast? Yes, yes! *(He tears open his shirt, picks up a knife, and points it at his chest.)*

MASTER: Put down that knife. *(He grabs it from his hand.)* Come, let's have a drink, and then I'll reveal the severe condition you must satisfy to win my pardon. . . . So Agathe is as passionate as she looks!

SAINT-OUEN: Ah, if only you could know her as I do!

JACQUES *(to* SAINT-OUEN*)*: Has she got long legs?

SAINT-OUEN *(to* JACQUES, *softly)*: Not particularly.

JACQUES: And a nice big bottom?

SAINT-OUEN *(the same)*: Flat as a board.

JACQUES *(to his* MASTER*)*: I see you are a dreamer, sir, and love you all the more for it.

MASTER *(to* SAINT-OUEN*)*: Let me state my condition. While we empty this bottle, I want you to talk to me about Agathe. You'll tell me what she's like in bed, what she says. How she moves. What she does. Her sighs. You'll tell me, we'll drink, and I'll imagine it. . . . *(*SAINT-OUEN *stares at the* MASTER *without responding.)* Well? Are you willing? What's the matter? Speak! *(*SAINT-OUEN *remains silent.)* Do you hear me?

SAINT-OUEN: I do.

MASTER: Do you agree?

SAINT-OUEN: I do.

MASTER: Then why don't you drink?

SAINT-OUEN: I'm looking at you.

MASTER: I can see that.

SAINT-OUEN: We're the same height. In the dark, one of us could easily be mistaken for the other.

MASTER: Well, and what of it? Why don't you start? I want to imagine it! Damn it all, Saint-Ouen, I can't wait! I want you to tell me now!

SAINT-OUEN: So you want me to describe a night with Agathe?

MASTER: You don't know what passion is! Yes, I want you to! Is that too much to ask?

SAINT-OUEN: On the contrary. It's a mere trifle. Indeed, what would you say if instead of describing the night, I gave you the night itself?

MASTER: The night itself? A real night?

SAINT-OUEN *(taking two keys from his pocket)*: The small one opens the front door; the large one, the door to Agathe's antechamber. I've been using them for six months, my friend. I stroll along the street until a potted basil plant appears in the window. I open the door of the house and close it quietly. Quietly I climb the stairs. Quietly I unlock her door. Off the antechamber is an alcove, where I undress. Agathe leaves the door to her bedchamber ajar and awaits me there in her bed, in the dark.

MASTER: And you'd let me take your place?

SAINT-OUEN: With all my heart. I have only one small request. . . .

MASTER: Name it!

SAINT-OUEN: May I?

MASTER: By all means. I want no more than to make you happy.

SAINT-OUEN: You're the best friend a man has ever had.

MASTER: No worse than you. Now then, what can I do for you?

SAINT-OUEN: I'd like you to remain in her arms until morning. Then I'll happen on the scene and surprise you.

MASTER *(with a rather shocked little laugh)*: Splendid idea! But isn't it a bit cruel?

SAINT-OUEN: Cruel? Not very. Droll, actually. I, too, shall undress in the alcove, and when I surprise you, I'll be . . .

MASTER: Naked! Oh, the perfect profligate! But how shall we manage? We've only one set of keys. . . .

SAINT-OUEN: We enter the house together, undress together in the alcove, but you go in to her first. Then as soon as you're ready, you give me a signal and I join you!

MASTER: An excellent idea! It's divine!

SAINT-OUEN: Then you agree?

MASTER: Of course! But . . .

SAINT-OUEN: But . . .

MASTER: But . . . You see, I . . . No, no, I agree without reservation. Except that, well, since this is the first time, I'd actually prefer to be alone with her. . . . Perhaps later we could . . .

SAINT-OUEN: Ah, I see. You intend to avenge us several times over.

MASTER: The revenge is so sweet . . .

SAINT-OUEN: How true. *(He nods upstage, where* AGATHE *is lying on a step. The* MASTER *moves toward her as if under a spell, and she holds her arms out to him.)* Careful! Quiet! The whole house is asleep! *(The* MASTER *lies down next to* AGATHE *and takes her in his arms. . . .)*

JACQUES: I congratulate you, sir, but I fear for you.

SAINT-OUEN *(from the platform, to* JACQUES*)*: According to all the rules, my friend, a servant should rejoice to see his master duped.

JACQUES: My master is a good fellow; he does as I say. I don't like to see other masters, not such good fellows, leading him by the nose.

SAINT-OUEN: Your master is a moron and deserves a moron's fate.

JACQUES: In some ways perhaps he is a fool. But there's a gentle wisdom to his follies, a wisdom I don't find in your cleverness.

SAINT-OUEN: Well, well! A servant enamored of his master! Watch closely and see what this adventure gets him!

JACQUES: In the meantime he's happy, and I'm happy for him!

SAINT-OUEN: We shall see!

JACQUES: In the meantime he's happy, I tell you, and that's good enough for me. What more can one ask than to be happy in the meantime?

SAINT-OUEN: Well, he'll pay dearly for his moment of happiness!

JACQUES: But what if his moment of happiness is so great that even all the misfortunes you've prepared for him will not outweigh it?

SAINT-OUEN: Hold your tongue, servant! If I thought I'd given your dolt of a master more pleasure than pain, I'd indeed run this knife through my heart. *(He calls upstage into the wings.)* Quickly, there! Quickly! It's nearly daybreak!

# Scene 3

*A great commotion is heard offstage. Then a group of people, including* AGATHE'S MOTHER *and* FATHER *in nightclothes, and the* POLICE OFFICER, *rush over to the step where the* MASTER *and* AGATHE *lie entwined.*

POLICE OFFICER: Quiet, ladies and gentlemen! The evidence is conclusive. Caught in the act. The culprit, if I am not mistaken, is an aristocrat and an honorable man. I trust he will right this wrong on his own rather than wait till the law constrains him to it.

JACQUES: Good God, sir, now they've got you where they want you.

AGATHE'S FATHER *(holding back* AGATHE'S MOTHER, *who is trying to beat* AGATHE*)*: Let her be! Everything will turn out for the best. . . .

AGATHE'S MOTHER *(to the* MASTER*)*: You seemed so honorable. Who'd have thought that you would . . .

POLICE OFFICER *(to the* MASTER, *who has in the meantime picked himself up from the step)*: Follow me, sir.

MASTER: And where do you propose to take me?

POLICE OFFICER *(leading him off)*: To prison.

JACQUES *(stunned)*: To prison?

MASTER *(to* JACQUES*)*: Yes, Jacques, my boy, to prison . . .

*(The* POLICE OFFICER *exits. The small group that had formed in the vicinity of the step disappears. The* MASTER *is alone on the platform.* SAINT-OUEN *rushes over to him.)*

SAINT-OUEN: Oh, my dear, dear friend! How perfectly frightful! You, in prison! How can it be? I've just now come from Agathe's. Her parents refuse to speak to me. They know you're my only friend and blame me for their misfortune. Agathe nearly scratched out my eyes. You understand her position. . . .

MASTER: You alone, Saint-Ouen, can get me out.

SAINT-OUEN: But how?

MASTER: How? By telling the truth.

SAINT-OUEN: Yes, and I've threatened Agathe to do just that. But I can't go through with it. Think of what we two would look like. . . . Besides, it's all your fault!

MASTER: My fault?

SAINT-OUEN: Yes, yours! If you had agreed to my little nastiness, Agathe would have been caught between two men, and she would have ended up the fool. You were too selfish, my friend! You had to have her all to yourself!

MASTER: Saint-Ouen!

SAINT-OUEN: That's how it is, my friend. You're being punished for your selfishness.

MASTER *(reproachfully)*: My friend!

*(SAINT-OUEN turns on his heel and exits.)*

JACQUES *(calling to the MASTER)*: Damn it all! When are you going to stop calling him your friend? Everybody knows that it was all a trap, that he was the one who denounced you! But no, you'll always be blind! And I'll be a laughingstock for having an imbecile for a master!

# Scene 4

MASTER *(turning toward* JACQUES *and stepping down from the platform during the speech)*: If only he were just an imbecile, Jacques, my boy. But he was unlucky besides, and that's worse. After I'd been released from prison, I had to cleanse their daughter's tainted honor with a considerable sum. . . .

JACQUES *(by way of consolation)*: It could have been still worse, sir. Supposing the girl had been pregnant.

MASTER: You've guessed it.

JACQUES: What?

MASTER: Yes.

JACQUES: She was knocked up? *(The* MASTER *nods, and* JACQUES *puts his arms around him.)* Master! My poor little master! Now I know the worst of endings of a story.

*(Throughout this scene, the dialogue between* JACQUES *and his* MASTER *is imbued with genuine sadness and is completely free of comedy.)*

MASTER: Not only did I pay for that little tart's tainted honor, I was ordered to pay for her confinement, to say nothing of the maintenance and upbringing of a little brat who is the repellent image of my friend Saint-Ouen.

JACQUES: Now I know. The worst of endings of a human story is a brat. The sinister full stop at the end of the adventure. The blot at the end of love. And how old is he now, your son?

MASTER: Nearly ten. He's been in a village all this time,

and I plan to stop off there on our travels, settle my account with the people keeping him, and have the little snot apprenticed.

JACQUES: Remember at the beginning when they *(he nods at the audience)* asked me where we were going and I answered,"Which of us knows where we're going?" Well, you knew all along, my sad little master.

MASTER: I think I'll make him a watchmaker. Or a carpenter. Yes, better a carpenter. He will make multitudes of chairs and multitudes of children and the children will make new chairs and new children who will beget new multitudes of children and chairs. . . .

JACQUES: And the world will be cluttered with chairs, and that will be your revenge.

MASTER *(with disgust)*: The grass will cease to grow, the flowers to bloom, and everywhere there will be only children and chairs.

JACQUES: Children and chairs, chairs and children. It's a grim picture you paint of the future. How lucky we are, sir! We'll die in time.

MASTER *(pensively)*: I certainly hope so, Jacques, because there are times when I feel great anxiety at the thought of the continual repetition of children and chairs and all that. . . . You know what I wondered yesterday evening as I listened to the story of Madame de La Pommeraye? Whether it isn't always one and the same story. After all, Madame de La Pommeraye is merely a replica of Saint-Ouen, while I am no more than a version of your poor friend Bigre, who himself is but a counterpart of that dupe of a Marquis. And I see no difference whatever between Justine and Agathe, and Agathe is the double of the little whore the Marquis eventually married.

JACQUES *(pensively)*: Yes, sir, it's like a merry-go-round.

You know, my grandfather, the one who kept me gagged and read the Bible every night, he didn't always like what he read, he would even say that the Bible repeated itself and that anyone who repeated himself took his listeners for idiots. And you know what I've been wondering, sir? Whether the one who does all the writing on high hasn't repeated himself an incredible amount and whether he, too, doesn't take us for idiots . . . (JACQUES *falls silent, and the* MASTER *is too sad to respond. After a pause,* JACQUES *tries to console him.*) But good God, sir, don't be so sad. What can I do to cheer you up? I know what, dear little Master. I'll tell you the story of how I fell in love.

MASTER *(in a melancholy voice)*: Yes, tell me, Jacques, my boy.

JACQUES: The day I lost my virginity, I went out and got drunk.

MASTER: Yes, I know.

JACQUES: Oh, I'm sorry. Then I'll skip ahead to the surgeon's wife.

MASTER: So she's the one you fell in love with?

JACQUES: No.

MASTER *(looking around with sudden suspicion)*: Well, then, skip her too, and go on quickly.

JACQUES: Why are you in such a hurry all of a sudden?

MASTER: Something tells me, Jacques, that we haven't much time.

JACQUES: Sir, you scare me.

MASTER: Something tells me you'd better be quick about finishing your story.

JACQUES: Very well, sir. After a week's rest at the surgeon's, I went out for a walk. *(*JACQUES *is absorbed in his story and looks more at the audience than at his* MASTER, *who becomes more and more interested in the countryside.)* It was a beautiful day, though I was still limping badly. . . .

MASTER: You know, Jacques, I think we're coming to the village where my bastard lives.

JACQUES: Sir, you're interrupting me at the most beautiful moment! I was still limping badly and my knee still throbbed, but it was a beautiful day, I can see it as if it were now. *(*SAINT-OUEN *appears at the edge of the stage. He does not see the* MASTER, *but the* MASTER *sees and stares at him.* JACQUES *is now completely absorbed in his story and looks straight out into the audience.)* It was autumn, sir, the trees were all different colors, the sky blue, and as I was walking along a path in the woods, I noticed a girl coming in my direction, and I'm very glad you haven't interrupted me, because it was a beautiful day and she was a beautiful girl, don't interrupt me now, sir, and as she walked toward me, slowly, slowly, I looked at her, and she looked at me, and I saw what a beautiful, melancholy face she had, sir, melancholy, it was, and so beautiful. . . .

SAINT-OUEN *(noticing the* MASTER *at last, taken aback)*: Oh, it's you, my friend. . . .

*(The* Master *draws his sword;* SAINT-OUEN *follows suit.)*

MASTER: Yes, it is I! Your friend, the best friend you ever had! *(He lunges at him, and they begin to duel.)* What are you doing here? Come to have a look at your son, eh? Come to see if he's plump enough? If I've been giving him enough to eat?

JACQUES *(following the duel in terror)*: Careful, sir! Watch out! *(Before long,* SAINT-OUEN, *run through by the* MASTER, *collapses.* JACQUES *leans over him.)* I think he's had it. Oh, sir, why did this have to happen?

*(*JACQUES *is still leaning over* SAINT-OUEN *when a group of* PEASANTS *rushes onstage.)*

MASTER: Quickly, Jacques! Run! *(He runs off.)*

# Scene 5

JACQUES *does not manage to escape. He is caught by several* PEASANTS, *who tie his hands behind his back. His hands bound, he stands at the edge of the stage while the* BAILIFF *looks him up and down.*

BAILIFF: Tell me, friend, what do you think of the prospect of being thrown into prison, tried, and hanged?

JACQUES: All I can tell you is what my captain used to tell me: Everything that happens here below is written first on high.

BAILIFF: A great truth . . . *(He and the* PEASANTS *exit slowly, leaving* JACQUES *alone for his monologue.)*

JACQUES: Now, the value of what is written on high—that's another matter entirely. Oh, Master! I'm going to the gallows because you fell in love with that idiot . Agathe. Where is the wisdom in that, Master? Now you'll never know how I fell in love. That beautiful, melancholy girl was a servant at the château, and then I too was hired as a servant there, but you'll never know the end of the story because I'm going to be hanged, her name was Denise and I loved her dearly, loved her as I never loved again, but we were together only a fortnight, can you imagine, sir, only a fortnight, a fortnight because my master at the time, who was both my master and hers, gave me to the Comte de Boulay, who then gave me to his elder brother, the Captain, who gave me to his nephew, the public prosecutor of Toulouse, who gave me to the Comte de Trouville, and the Comte de Trouville gave me to the Marquise du Belloy, who ran off to London with an Englishman, which caused quite a scandal, but just before fleeing she took the time to commend me to the Capitaine de Marty, yes, sir, the very captain who used to say that everything was written on high, and he gave me to Monsieur Hérissant, who placed me with Mademoiselle Isselin, whom you, sir, were keeping at the time, but who got on your nerves because she was lean and hysterical, and whenever she got on your nerves I would make you laugh with my chatter, so you took a liking to me and would certainly have provided for me in my old age, because you promised to, and I know you'd have kept your word, we'd never have parted, we were made for each other. Jacques for his master, his master for Jacques. And here we are, separated, and for such a stupid prank! Good God, what do I care if you let that scoundrel get the better of you! Why must I hang for your good heart and bad taste! The stupidities written on high! Oh, Master, he who wrote our story on high must have been a very bad poet, the worst of bad poets, the king, the emperor of bad poets!

*(During* Jacques's *last few lines,* Young Bigre *appears at the edge of the stage. He stands staring at him questioningly, then calls to him.)*

Young Bigre: Jacques?

Jacques *(without looking at him)*: Shove off, damn you!

Young Bigre: Is that you, Jacques?

Jacques: Shove off, all of you! I'm talking to my master!

Young Bigre: Damn it, Jacques, don't you recognize me? *(He grabs hold of* Jacques *and turns him round to face him.)*

JACQUES: Bigre . . .

YOUNG BIGRE: Why are your hands tied?

JACQUES: They're going to hang me.

YOUNG BIGRE: Hang you? No . . . My friend! Fortunately there are still friends around who don't forget their friends! *(He undoes the rope binding* JACQUES's *hands, swings him round to face him again, and puts his arms around him. They are still embracing when* JACQUES *bursts out laughing.)* What are you laughing about?

JACQUES: Here I was, telling off a bad poet for being such a bad poet, and what does he do but quickly send me you to correct his bad poem. And I tell you, Bigre, even the worst of poets couldn't have come up with a more cheerful ending for his bad poem!

YOUNG BIGRE: I don't understand a word you're saying, my friend, but it doesn't matter! I've never forgotten you. Remember the attic? *(Now it is his turn to laugh. He gives* JACQUES *a slap on the back.* JACQUES *laughs with him.)* Do you see it? *(He points upstage to the attic.)* That's no attic, my boy! It's a chapel! It's a temple of true friendship! You have no idea, Jacques, how happy you made us! You enlisted in the army, remember? And, well, a month later I found out that Justine . . . *(He pauses significantly.)*

JACQUES: What about her?

YOUNG BIGRE: That Justine . . . *(he makes another eloquent pause)* . . . was going to have . . . *(He pauses once more.)* Well, guess! . . . A baby.

JACQUES: And it was a month after I enlisted that you found out about it?

YOUNG BIGRE: What could my father say? He had no choice but to let me marry her. And eight months later . . . *(He makes an eloquent pause.)*

JACQUES: What was it?

YOUNG BIGRE: A boy!

JACQUES: How is he doing?

YOUNG BIGRE *(proudly)*: Fine, just fine! We named him Jacques in your honor! And believe it or not, he even looks a little like you. You'll have to come and see him! Justine will be thrilled!

JACQUES *(looking back)*: Dear little Master, our stories look laughably alike. . . . *(*YOUNG BIGRE *leads him off with great glee.)*

# *Scene 6*

MASTER *(entering the bare stage and calling out unhappily)*: Jacques! Jacques, my boy! *(He looks around.)* Ever since I lost you, the stage is as bare as the world and the world as bare as an empty stage. . . . What I wouldn't give to hear you tell the fable of the Knife and the Sheath again. That disgusting fable. Then I could reject and renounce it and declare it null and void, and you could tell it again and tell it each time as if it were the first. . . . Oh, Jacques, my boy, if only I could reject the story of Saint-Ouen like that! . . . But only your wonderful stories can be revoked; my stupid intrigue is irrevocable. And I'm in it by myself, without you and the splendid asses you evoked with your sweet rambling lips. . . . *(He dreamily recites the following line as if it were from an ode.)* Hail, voluptuous rumps! Hail, resplendent full moons! . . . *(In his usual voice.)* You were right, you know. None of us knows where we're going. I thought I'd have a look at my bastard, and instead lost my dear little Jacques.

JACQUES (*coming up to the* MASTER *from the other side*): My little Master . . .

MASTER (*turning toward* JACQUES, *amazed*): Jacques!

JACQUES: Remember what that noble female of an innkeeper with the big bottom said about us: We can't live without each other. (*The* MASTER *is overcome with emotion. He falls into* JACQUES*'s arms, and* JACQUES *comforts him.*) There, there. Now tell me, where are we going?

MASTER: Which of us knows where we're going?

JACQUES: Nobody knows.

MASTER: No one.

JACQUES: You lead the way, then.

MASTER: How can I lead the way if we don't know where we're going?

JACQUES: Because it's written on high. You are my master and it's your duty to lead.

MASTER: True, but haven't you forgotten what's written a bit farther on? That the master gives the orders, but Jacques chooses among them. Well? I'm waiting!

JACQUES: All right, then. I want you to lead me . . . forward. . . .

MASTER (*looking around, highly embarrassed*): Very well, but where is forward?

JACQUES: Let me tell you a great secret. One of mankind's oldest tricks. Forward is anywhere.

MASTER (*turning his head round in a circle*): Anywhere?

JACQUES (*making a large circle with one arm*): Anywhere you look, it's all forward!

MASTER (*without enthusiasm*): Why, that's splendid,

Jacques! That's splendid! *(He turns around slowly in place.)*

JACQUES *(melancholy)*: Yes, sir. I find it quite wonderful myself.

MASTER *(after a brief bit of stage business, sadly)*: Well then, Jacques, forward!

*(They exit diagonally upstage. . . .)*

*Prague, July 1971*